About the Author

Jane Allen is the author of the acclaimed Hollywood biography, Pier Angeli: A Fragile Life (McFarland & Co. 2002). She has worked as a cook and art gallery director and has a Master of Philosophy from Sydney University. She has travelled extensively and was once trapped in India for six weeks during a border dispute with China. She is passionate about researching her family history, collects antique jewelry, and lives in Bowral, Australia.

The Impassioned Collector

Jane Allen

The Impassioned Collector

Olympia Publishers
London

www.olympiapublishers.com
OLYMPIA PAPERBACK EDITION

Copyright © Jane Allen 2024

The right of Jane Allen to be identified as author of
this work has been asserted in accordance with sections 77 and 78 of the Copyright,
Designs and Patents Act 1988.

All Rights Reserved

No reproduction, copy or transmission of this publication
may be made without written permission.
No paragraph of this publication may be reproduced,
copied or transmitted save with the written permission of the publisher, or in accordance with the provisions
of the Copyright Act 1956 (as amended).

Any person who commits any unauthorised act in relation to
this publication may be liable to criminal
prosecution and civil claims for damage.

A CIP catalogue record for this title is
available from the British Library.

ISBN: 978-1-80074-458-5

First Published in 2024

Olympia Publishers
Tallis House
2 Tallis Street
London
EC4Y 0AB

Printed in Great Britain

Dedication

For the grandchildren

Acknowledgements

It is a gift for any biographer to have family approval and this book could not have been written without it.

My heartfelt thanks are due first to Harry and Kim Bradshaw for their hospitality, unlimited access to fourteen family photo albums and most importantly, the inventory of Arthur Bradshaw's Fabergé et al collection.

Vivien Stals, a granddaughter with considerable research skills and an interest in family history, and her husband Martin, have been a major support throughout the writing of this book. They offered hospitality, information, unlimited and constant encouragement, and Martin heroically scanned, transposed, enlarged and upgraded all the photo albums, the content of which supplied over half the information in the book.

Patricia and Robert Sharp offered hospitality, a revealing interest in family history, and shared their photos. Sara and Robin Stephenson shared hospitality, and an interesting silver dish. Jim Bradshaw, a family archivist, was always available for checking sources and details of family history. Richard Bradshaw (an American cousin, possessor of a huge archive of Bradshaw material and author of several books of family history) started the whole thing by sending me photos of two Fabergé objects owned by Arthur, that appeared in the Forbes Collection auction catalogue. Martin Lipson, who lives in The Grange and is the Steeple Aston archivist, has been an invaluable source of Grange history. SAVA Steeple Aston Village Archive was used extensively.

It was my good fortune to meet Richard and Daphne Preston towards the end of writing. They live within the grounds of The

Grange. A grandson of the original head gardener Dick Wadham, Richard is in possession of valuable family letters and information about The Grange as it was then, and is now, in particular the gardens, and was happy to show me around. Charlotte Sale generously shared information about the Sale family.

All the above are either grandchildren, other relatives, or are closely connected to The Grange. I am deeply grateful to them all. Living in Australia has meant that most of my initial information was gathered on two trips to England, thereafter I relied upon the goodwill of the family and others to supply the rest. My grateful thanks are due to Linda Tobey for her assistance in organising a Readers' ticket for the libraries in London containing essential Fabergé literature, and other encouragement. Christel Ludewig McCanless, noted Fabergé scholar, author of Fabergé and his Works: an annotated bibliography of the first century of his Art and publisher of a quarterly Fabergé Newsletter, kindly edited the chapter on the Collection and saved me from making several, possibly fatal, errors. She has been a tower of strength and support from the beginning and I am forever indebted to her scholarship.

At Wartski, initially Geoffrey Munn and latterly Kieran McCarthy have been encouraging, kind, and exceptionally generous in sharing their expertise. Geoffrey sent me his amazing book where Arthur heads the chapter on Collecting, and Kieran has, amongst other things, uncovered fakes in Arthur's collection, to which I was blind, lending authenticity to the manuscript. Denny Stone, Senior Collections Manager at the Metropolitan Museum of Art, New York, gave me access to a photograph of Arthur's Fabergé cigarette case, following permission from the Matilda Geddings Gray Collection. I am most grateful for the kind assistance of the following contributors at The Royal Collection: Caroline de Guitaut, Karen Lawson, and Daniel Partridge. Thanks are also due to Sofia Grigoryeva of the Fabergé Museum, St. Petersburg, for facilitating permission to reproduce items from their collection, also to Roy Tomlin for Romanov Tercentenary information.

My Australian editor Pamela Hewitt, has as always, encouraged me and guided this book into being. Always a tower of strength and support, it could not have been written without her. My gratitude is boundless."

A big thank you is also due to Kristina Smith at Olympia for her guidance during the publishing process.

All photographs, unless otherwise specified, are from the Collection of Harry and Kim Bradshaw.

TABLE OF CONTENTS

1935	15
1879	19
1899	34
1900	39
1904	51
1905	54
1908	70
1914	78
1915	88
1917	110
1929-31	137
1938	168
1939	171
The Collection	178
The Coronation Box (1897)	183
The Coronation Egg (1897)	185
The Bay Tree Egg (1911)	189
Nicholas II Equestrian Egg (1913)	195
Basket of Lilies of Valley (1896)	203
Spray of Cornflowers, Buttercups, and a Diamond Bee (c.1900)	207
Bibliography	214
Journals and Catalogues	215
Family notes	216

Arthur Bradshaw portrait

1935

Nothing will turn a man's home into a castle more quickly and effectively than a dachshund.

Queen Victoria

On a crisp February morning Arthur Bradshaw ambled along Piccadilly thinking about dog collars; he had six dachshunds at home and some of their accoutrements were looking a bit shabby. Bright light from a clean-washed blue sky was suddenly blocked with fast moving, cotton-wool clouds, darkening the morning, and emitting the occasional flurry of snow. Arthur turned up his collar, adjusted the brim of his hat and closed his eyes against the stinging flakes. He had no destination in mind. His mood was content. He had stayed in London overnight and entertained some friends from South Africa at his club in St James's. Now he had a few hours to kill before his train and he fancied wandering London.

At the bottom of the Burlington Arcade, he crossed the road, buffeted by the wind, and paused at Hatchards. The Christmas best-sellers were still displayed in one window. In the other was a poster advertising a conversation with an author and a book signing, the cover showing snow-capped mountains and a man leaning on an alpenstock. A mountaineer, Arthur thought, how very daring. He sheltered in the doorway and lit a cigarette, then found himself staring at the photograph of the author and imagined he saw fear in the man's eyes.

Dropping the match on the pavement, he hurried up the street. At

Piccadilly Circus he hesitated. He could turn right and go to the National Gallery, or head into Soho, but it was too early for lunch.

On impulse, he turned left and headed up Regent Street, the weather now behind him. He wasn't looking at anything in particular, but a sudden flash caught his eye and he found himself drawn to a shop window. It was a jeweller, not one he had seen before. He followed the source of the light to a bracelet displayed in a velvet-lined box. Diamonds and onyx. Very pretty indeed, thought Arthur, who knew something about diamonds, having wintered in South Africa on occasion with the Cullinan family. In fact, one of his guests the previous evening had been a diamond merchant and this morning he would be in Hatton Gardens with his pocketful of gems that he had shown to the assembled company at dinner. Arthur had not been tempted by the stones. He'd brought a few back sometimes for Evelyn but she didn't really care for jewels. He glanced up to read the name Wartski above the window and the number one hundred and thirty-eight on the door.

He was about to move on when a sudden thought struck. It was his eldest daughter Loveday's birthday soon. She would be twenty and he should mark the occasion with something grownup. He looked again at the bracelet and, dog collars forgotten, he stepped up to the door. It was instantly swung open by an invisible hand.

He found himself in a warm, brightly lit Aladdin's cave. Treasures sparkled on every table and shelf.

Arthur removed his hat, drew a deep breath, and coughed. A dapper man with a bow tie and sleek dark hair emerged from a shadow at the back of the shop. He regarded large, wind-rumpled Arthur and inclined his head.

"Good morning, sir, I am Emanuel Snowman, proprietor of Wartski. May I show you something?"

He offered Arthur a cigarette from a gold case. Arthur took one and smiled his thanks.

"I have a daughter with a birthday in April," he said, "and I was admiring a bracelet in your window."

Snowman slid back the glass and reached in.

"This one?" He pointed to the onyx and Arthur nodded. He took the bracelet from the box and laid it carefully on a black velvet cloth he had whisked from below the counter. Arthur picked it up and turned it over. It was exquisitely made and the diamonds of first quality. He put it down and turned to a table with a display of gold and jewelled snuff boxes.

"You have beautiful things," he said.

Snowman smiled. "Thank you, sir. Yes, we do. Those boxes are from Russia and some of them belonged to the late Tsar and his unfortunate family." He lowered his eyes discreetly.

Arthur moved to a shelf where a carved figure of a man sitting cross-legged and playing a guitar of sorts caught his attention. Arthur stared. This was not a toy. He did not know quite what it was, but it was not a china ornament such as his mother might have kept on her bureau, and it was in a jeweller's shop. There was something so immensely appealing about the carving that he felt a compulsion unknown to him and could barely restrain himself from touching the little figure.

"What is this?"

Snowman picked it off the shelf and put it beside the bracelet.

"This is a hardstone carving of a typical Russian type, a balalaika player, by Carl Fabergé. A master jeweller of St Petersburg, maker of Easter eggs and other jewels for the Imperial family, now sadly all gone." He did not ask Arthur if he had heard of Fabergé.

"The Russian government has need of money to rebuild the economy after the Revolution and they are selling some of their national treasures from the Armory in Moscow," he continued. "We have been privileged to be able to obtain some for our shop."

Arthur handed Snowman his card.

"You can send your account to me at this address. I shall take the figure and the bracelet," said Arthur, smitten.

Later, on the train, he wondered why he had not thought to ask the price.

In his Regent Street establishment, Emanuel Snowman was wondering the same thing. Arthur Bradshaw had appeared from nowhere, not just a stranger sheltering from the weather, but a man with an eye for a diamond bracelet and clearly a gentleman, despite his ill-fitting clothes. He had spent £350. Snowman looked at the card. He had never heard of Steeple Aston. He could travel from London to Moscow with his eyes closed but had no knowledge of the geography of Oxfordshire.

I wonder if I will ever see him again, he mused, and rather hoped he would.

That purchase, on 2nd February 1935, was a matter of pure chance, if one believes there is such a thing as chance. Indeed, it was a fateful encounter and it dealt Arthur such a coup de foudre that the fever lasted for the rest of his life.

1879

The man stood at the window watching a badger nose its way across the garden in the gathering dusk. A light snow had fallen during the day and little drifts had settled on the lawn. Won't last, thought the man as the badger stopped and was digging determinedly. *Hungry I expect.* It had been a hard winter.

In the room behind him he could hear a faint clucking, as Emma, his wife of seventeen years, attended to their last-born son, Arthur Edward, now a year old. Five sons, two daughters, that's enough now.

It would soon be time for the sailor to come home from the sea.

In the distance he could just see a faint glow as the gas lamps in the marketplace of Abingdon were lit. I like it here. I could retire here to Tubney, or anywhere in Oxfordshire where it is green and peaceful. When the time comes, I want to live as far from the sea as possible.

He watched the badger, now scrabbling furiously at something – grubs or a frog perhaps. It was almost too dark to see. He thought, suddenly, of his brother Henry. He looked a bit like a badger. Henry was a scholar, a clever chap, Dean of King's College, Cambridge, unmarried, and with little in common with his brothers. Henry didn't care much for children, only books really, and they hardly saw him.

Then his thoughts drifted to his other brother, Thomas, to whom he was close. He was now a judge, married to pretty Emily with ten children between them but three of their four sons cruelly dead too young. Thomas, whom he had seen at their sister Mary Charlotte's wedding recently, was still grieving for little Humphrey who died in a nursery accident, and Victor, the eldest, a naval cadet, had been with

Richard in South Africa, killed during a battle with the Ashanti. He'd had to write to Thomas with the tragic news. Wilfred, the third child, had died young of consumption. Thomas had taken these deaths very hard indeed, and now there was just Hugh, a mite overprotected in Richard's opinion and still at home at thirteen but, he thought ruefully, *if I had lost three sons I would probably be the same.*

Henry and Thomas were sent to Eton, while he had been at naval academy. *We brothers did well,* thought Richard. *Top of our professions.*

Then he checked himself. Boasting was bad form and in truth, although awarded the Order of the Bath and the South African Medal just before Christmas for his gallant action in the diverting his ship HMS Shah to assist in the Zulu wars, where his timely action undoubtedly averted a massacre, he was just a plain, seafaring man with simple tastes.

A man of few words, Richard was square-faced, with a firm jaw and horizon-seeking eyes. The new art of photography had not appealed to the brothers and both Richard and Thomas looked nervous and uncomfortable in their formal portraits. There is no known photograph of Henry, just an etching showing an aesthetic badger profile and the same down-turned mouth as his brothers.

His reverie was interrupted by a wailing from the next room that returned him to the present evening. Arthur was awake. *Why did we call him Arthur?* he wondered. There is nobody of that name on his side of the family, must have been a fancy of Emma's. He peered into the gloom, but the badger was no longer to be seen. Time for a tot before dinner.

Squaring his shoulders, he descended to the library. Settling with a satisfying creak into his favourite old leather chair, Richard picked up an illustrated paper and started reading the story of a disaster on the Thames a few months ago, when the passenger paddle steamer *SS*

Princess Alice, overloaded with day trippers, had been cut in half and sunk by the *SS Bywell Castle* with the loss of six hundred and fifty lives. Some had died later as the result of gulping heavily polluted water from the sewerage outfall. The Captain of the *Bywell Castle* was Thomas Harrison.

Richard sat up straight as he read the name. Harrison was a friend. He read further with growing concern as more details of the tragedy were revealed; Harrison, he knew, was a master mariner and part owner of the ship. A Board of Trade Inquiry had exonerated him, but Richard knew such a catastrophe was not one a man would swiftly get over. He would be constantly haunted, he thought, his health might suffer. I must write to him.

Despite Richard's comforting letter, Harrison's health broke down completely and he never returned to the sea, and in 1883 the ill-fated *Bywell Castle* disappeared with all hands off the coast of Portugal.

***

The Bradshaws were not a rich family. However, two of the boys were educated at Eton, and all three had made their way in the world.

In 1879 Richard Bradshaw's annual salary as a Captain was £1,460. He had five sons to educate. He married well. His wife Emma Walker, small but imperious, came from the Taylor Walker Brewery family and had substantial means. Emma was short, in her youth slim, and she moved energetically. Age and seven children robbed her of her neat waistline, but she had a truly sweet expression that captivated all who met her, and pretty hands she enhanced by wearing wide white cuffs on all her silks. She was also an exceptionally strong character. Her motto, which she instilled into her children, was "you can accomplish anything if you put your mind to it."

Hard work brought the Walker family substantial wealth. Emma's great grandfather, Isaac Walker, had been a prosperous linen merchant, a Quaker, and noted collector of mineral specimens – more for their beauty than for scientific interest. The collection is now in the Natural History Museum in South Kensington. Isaac had been a philanthropist in his way; buying up food and selling it cheaply to the poor. His eldest son John opened a charity school in 1812. He and his wife Sally had ten children. The eldest, Isaac, married Sophia Taylor and had twelve children, seven sons who famously played cricket and never married, and five daughters, all of whom did marry and one of whom was Emma.

The Taylor Walker Brewery partnership was founded in 1816. The brewery at Limehouse on the Thames was known as the Limehouse brewery, until it expanded in 1889 with a substantial new brewery being added on to the existing building and the name changed to the Barley Mow Brewery.

The Walker brothers gave generously to around one hundred charities and Edward Vyell, local councillor and the best all-round cricketer until the legendary Dr W.G. Grace, gave fourteen acres of pasture to the village for a recreation ground in perpetuity, and he paid for the fences and gates while the villagers raised the funds for a pavilion. The Walker Cricket Ground is maintained to this day by the Walker Trust.

The charitable instinct was strongly present in Emma's nature. She was of a kindly disposition and her philanthropy, wherever she lived, and particularly towards the village of Steeple Aston and her poorer neighbours, was an example to her children and a tradition that John, Stewart, and Arthur would follow in their turn. She was the matriarch of the Bradshaw family, and the embodiment of a good woman.

Richard's dream of retirement to Oxfordshire was not to be realised for another three years. Shortly after the badger sighting, the navy sent him to Devonport in Cornwall to captain the training ship

Impregnable. He was obliged to take a house nearby for his burgeoning family and the retinue required to look after it.

Thanckes House in Torpoint, home of the Graves family, was available, fitted the bill and was leased for the duration. A country house with a substantial landscape, Thanckes was further ornamented in the eighteenth century by Rear-Admiral Thomas Graves, who created a small park. The main elements were two avenues running from the original house on either side of large lawn with a scattering of standard trees and a wonderful quarry garden. The house itself had been recently demolished in 1871 and replaced with another one, set within one of the former house's two large walled gardens.

Emma had a staff of ten, transferring the children's nurse, Mary Horsegood, as well as four family retainers from Tubney and taking on half a dozen locals, thereby giving employment to the inhabitants and profiting from their homegrown knowledge.

Richard knew that at the age of sixty Devonport was his last posting, so he started putting out feelers for a house in Oxfordshire and before long he received word of an interesting manor house available in the village of Steeple Aston.

It is easy to miss the turning to Steeple Aston. Off the B4030, just over a small bridge; in summer the sign is hidden by foliage. The village, some seventeen miles from Oxford, is folded into a hill above the River Cherwell. It is mentioned in the Doomsday Book and has existed certainly since Roman times; a burial ground suggests there may have been a settlement in the Iron Age. To the north of the village, on a corner of the high ground stands the parish church of St Peter and St Paul, a listed building. The earliest recording of the church is 1180, with many alterations and additions over the centuries. Ancient headstones are scattered in the grass around the church and it has a tower rather than a steeple. Many of the Bradshaws are buried here.

Richard and Emma stood at the wrought iron gates looking through bare black branches of trees to The Grange. It was Christmas time and Richard had ten days leave. Snow lay on the ground and had piled up on one side of the big house, collected in little mounds on the balustrade and steps leading to the Tudor-arched front door. A low, slanting sun caught the upper part of the crenelated roof, picking out details of the pediments and gilding the cornices, lower down casting shadows on the caryatids, friezes, and architraves.

Emma breathed deeply. "A castle," she said, "like something from a fairy tale." Richard stared, somewhat bewildered but not yet feeling the magic. He was by now used to the big houses Emma had leased for their growing family, but this was something outside his experience. And was Emma suggesting it was to be their permanent home?

"It looks thrown together," he said. "Bit of a mix of architecture styles, rather mad don't you think?" But it is in exactly the right spot, he thought, and there is substantial land with woodland on the title. He could almost see smoke coming from the many chimneys. Then he bent down and scooped up a handful of snow, moulded it into a ball and threw it at the nearest tree where it exploded satisfactorily.

Emma smiled to herself; this was the playful Richard she loved and almost nobody else ever saw. He does like it, she thought. I think we have found a home.

Richard bought The Grange from Edward John Eyre, noted for his intrepid explorations of Australia; governance of New Zealand and Jamaica; and the scandal that surrounded his arrest and trial for murder and his subsequent acquittal. He left Steeple Aston in 1881 and retired to live in seclusion in Devon where he died twenty years later.

Prior to Eyre's occupation it had been the home of Thomas Davis, and it was he who created the present house. Trained as a doctor, he and his wife Maria settled in London where he had his practice. Then, when his aunt died in 1816, the family home in Steeple Aston was left to him. Davis established a country residence there and started a family. In due course he became a "royal" surgeon to King William IV. He is listed in the Court records held in Windsor as "Surgeon Extraordinary", one of the junior members of the medical team attending the monarch.

At some point Davis apparently acquired lots of decorative and other building materials from the Castellated Palace at Kew, designed by James Wyatt for William IV's father the mad King George. This extravagant building took decades to construct but was eventually demolished in about 1828 without ever having been occupied. Thomas allegedly incorporated these materials into his considerable expansion of The Grange. There is no documented evidence for this, however the ornamentations suggest that some of the materials indeed came from the Castellated Palace.

The Grange was an extraordinary and cumbersome house. Described by Pevsner in *The Buildings of Oxfordshire* as "an eccentric, ornamental castle" (p.787), it was originally built around 1720 as a modest country house, but with substantial grounds which, over time, were developed into a small country estate. Around 1824 Thomas started to alter and expand the house and the work appears to have continued for up to twenty years. This included: outbuildings, the dairy, stables, and the head gardener's cottage. All were carried out in a highly decorated Georgian Gothick style, then much in fashion. The house was the crowning glory of the estate, the additions doubling its size, with battlements, gothic windows of all shapes and sizes, and most particularly sculptures, gargoyles and friezes incorporated into the brick and stonework inside and outside.

Such a place would have been paradise for the seven Bradshaw children – the boys playing war games, the girls imprisoned princesses waiting to be rescued from the battlements.

Richard retired with the rank of Captain in January 1883 and over the next eight years rose, first to the rank of Rear Admiral in 1885, and finally to Vice Admiral in 1891. This is explained by an Act of Parliament which enabled Officers to gain promotion after retirement because the Navy was so huge at that point, and top heavy with senior Officers, junior ranks were not able to move up.

He acquired The Grange in 1881 but did not move in with his family for another two years. When they settled there in 1883, he set about finding anyone who had worked there in the past and giving them back their employment. The estate of some twenty-eight acres, as shown on a map of 1876, already had a kitchen garden, a formal garden, and a well-planted border of trees around the perimeter. Stables and cottages are also marked on this map and a pond. Gardeners, a coachman, cowman, stable hand, and groundsmen were taken on and the cottages were filled again, and Emma made inquiries in the village for a cook, kitchen and housemaids.

Richard became a magistrate for the county and an alderman for Oxford, and Emma tended to the children, ran the household and occupied herself with good works in the parish, gave to charity, and visited the sick.

Today, Steeple and Middle Aston have thirty-seven listed buildings and structures, including The Grange, home to the Bradshaw family for three generations over seventy years.

**

Richard and Emma had five sons and he spread their education between four different prep schools. Some were chosen for proximity to where they were living, others for a possible career.

John, the eldest, went to Radley College, between Oxford and Abingdon. Founded in 1847, it was inspired by the Oxford Movement and based on the Christian principles of brotherliness. Each boy had his own space. There was a daily choral service in the fine chapel, and the school had extensive playing fields, woodlands, and a lake. It sounds idyllic.

Richard, known as Stewart, and Joseph, known as Harry, were sent to Stubbington House, founded in 1841 and known as "the cradle of the navy" and both followed John to Radley.

However, none was destined for the navy as the Walker brothers – apart from Vyell Edward and Russell Donnithorne – spent more time playing cricket than running the brewery, which in the normal course of events would have been their inheritance, so Emma despatched three of her sons to the family concern.

Robert, happily known as Bob, for some reason was sent to Sandhurst from 1841, The Royal Military Academy where boys were trained "for excellence in leadership". John, Stewart, and Bob went to the Taylor Walker Brewery, Harry to the gold fields of Witwatersrand, and Arthur, after a short few years at Summertown school, St. Giles' Oxford, entered the navy at fourteen for what was to be a brief career.

John, the eldest, went to the brewery in 1885 at the age of twenty-two. He married his cousin Mary Kathleen Walker four years later and they lived thereafter in the small village of Southgate at The Grange, a country house with huge and very beautiful private gardens behind high walls. A shy, modest, and endlessly generous man, his benevolence was distributed quietly and often anonymously. He took public transport to and from the brewery.

"Where is he going?" Arthur asked Mary as he watched his brother setting off on a Saturday morning carrying a large straw bag.

"He is going to the Almshouses." She came and stood beside Arthur at the window and they watched John making his way down the road, head bent into the wind, tugging at his scarf. "He goes every Saturday; he always walks, and he takes little cakes and fruit from the garden to the old folk, food that they don't often see. They love him and look forward so much to his weekly visits – and he is very fond of them. He knows everyone in the village too, sometimes his walks take quite a long time as he always stops to talk."

Arthur nodded. "He is a good man. We'd all do well to follow his example."

"But you do," protested Mary. "You are involved with the Masons, you give to charity, you are a churchwarden like John, and you open your garden to the villagers and for the flower show… How long can you stay?"

"Just until tomorrow I'm afraid, I have to be in Oxford on Monday. I'd like to go round the garden with John after lunch if you don't have plans."

"No, we don't," she said, "I know he has set aside the rest of the weekend for you and he'd like you to go with him to the Southgate cricket club tomorrow afternoon to watch a match."

"I'd be delighted. Always happy to watch cricket, and to play; but not here of course, way above my standard."

She smiled, knowing he was thinking of his uncles and the twenty-five years the Walker brothers had dominated the cricket world, giving the land of Chapel Fields to Southgate village as a cricket ground, amongst other benefactions.

In the afternoon the brothers walked around the garden, John puffing on his pipe and pointing out plants that were of special interest to him. He had studied horticulture for a long time and knew Latin names and a great deal about the gardens and grounds around his Grange. "Father left your garden in good order, did he not? You must keep it up. It is the best place to shed the cares of the world. I am thinking I should open mine to other people as you do for the annual flower show."

"That was part of the inheritance," said Arthur, "the flower show was a big event in Dad's time. I know nothing about the plants, leave all that to Dick Wadham. Splendid man. I'm now renovating the bowling green for the village to play on. It's been neglected for years – been there since before Dad bought The Grange – and I'm thinking of putting in a pavilion."

John looked at him in surprise. "I didn't know you played bowls."

"I took it up when I retired from cricket. That was a Cape Town indulgence, along with golf which I still play a bit. It will be good for the village I think, and I plan to form a club, get other villages involved. I've just been asked to be the president of the Oxford Bowling Association. What would you open your garden for?"

"I've been thinking of having members of the Barley Mow sports club," said John. "I'm president now and I should entertain them at home at least once a year. Also, the Southgate Social Club have expressed interest in seeing my garden, as well as the Conservative Association."

"Come one, come all," murmured Arthur. A bit louder he said, "It all looks splendid, anyone would feel privileged to be invited inside your high walls."

John rose to become Chairman and President of the brewery in 1906. He spent his life at Southgate, never travelled abroad and seldom returned to Steeple Aston except for important family occasions. He and Mary Kathleen had no children. In the 1930s he watched, with dismay, the development of his village, in particular the building of large, semi-detached houses, and the famous art deco tube station opposite his house designed by Charles Holden and based on the Stockholm public library. It was dubbed "the flying saucer".

Arthur had indeed renovated the bowling green. On his return from South Africa and following his marriage, he settled at The Grange and set about managing the small estate. The large vegetable garden was in good shape, thanks to Emma, and it fed the family and their staff. Also, the extensive rose beds and borders had been lovingly maintained, but the bowling green had lapsed into a matted state as nobody was interested in playing on it. Dick Wadham had kept it mown, but that was all.

"What needs to be done to bring it back?" Arthur asked Dick as they stood by the wall, the sun warming their backs. Dick removed his hat and rubbed his head while he contemplated the square of grass.

"Probably needs to be re-seeded. It's a bit lumpy but it's level enough." Dick was known privately in some quarters as 'dead eye'. "Reckon the drainage needs seeing to and the edges are raggedy, so first a good raking over to get rid of the matting, that'll take care of the bumps and give it a bit of an airing."

"Let's do it then, and by next summer, come the flower show, perhaps we can add a bowling tournament to the general entertainment."

Dick looked at Arthur; he must know there's a war on, he thought, and probably no time to be having a flower show, but he made allowances, Dick did, and so he said nothing, but set about bringing the bowling green back to life. The bowling tournaments became one of the most popular attractions at the annual flower shows, when they resumed in the 1920s. There was a local team, and a Steeple Aston club with photos of Arthur sitting in the centre, front row, holding the cup which he undoubtedly had donated.

Richard Stewart – known as Stewart to his family, "Bradder" to his friends and Uncle Cuckoo to the children – was, by all accounts, a gambler, a good all-round sportsman and a cheery soul. A tall man, he had a habit of running his hands through his hair. He was an oarsman at school and retained his interest in the practice of rowing all his life, taking part in the Grand Challenge Cup at Henley over several years, and was also a steward of the regatta. He was a member of the London Rowing Club. Elected president in 1935 he served in that office until his death. He was a social golfer, and a keen racing man who hardly ever missed a meeting at Newmarket, Epsom or Ascot.

Stewart, too, went to the brewery, became a director and married Clara Aston in 1905. He sailed the following year to New York on the *SS Oceanic*, where, strangely, he was listed on the ship's manifest as "single." Happily, there are several photos of them both at The Grange, him mostly with Clarie, as she was called, a pleasant looking woman who seemed to be enjoying herself in the pictures taken on holidays and at the Steeple Aston Flower Show. They lived in Whyteleaf, Surrey where he was a generous supporter of all the welfare work of the parish church. There were no children.

When it comes to Robert, little is known about him but there is quite detailed information about his wife Doreen Marjorie O'Beirne, thanks to the happy circumstance that her childhood album was preserved in the Bradshaw archive. Born in 1886, Doreen's father was a major in the Royal Warwickshire Regiment. They lived at Lower Astrop, Kings Sutton, near Banbury. There were two sisters and a brother. Doreen is pictured aged four, sitting side-saddle on a horse called Beauty. The childhood appeared perfect; there were ponies, dogs, and holidays at Margate. Doreen kept everything important to her: dance programmes, playbills, concerts, and cards, her second-grade violin certificate and her watercolours of dogs and churches, which are charming. She had her handwriting analysed by a London graphologist. Not content with his scrutiny, she had it done again (by the same person, a rather naïve attempt to gain a better character) with an almost identical result. She was told she was "lively, genial, very good natured, intelligent, clear-headed, self-possessed, energetic, outspoken, loyal, cheerful and friendly". If she had faults, they were minor: a lack of order, incaution, and impatience.

A serious child in the early photos, there is barely a hint of the extraordinarily pretty woman who would marry Bob. The first intimation of her beauty is a photo taken in 1903, aged seventeen, with a rather plain friend, showing a tiny waist and a lovely face.

Bob appears in a newspaper report of her father's party at a Hunt Ball the year in 1907, followed by their engagement at Christmas and the wedding in February, reported in detail in the *Banbury Guardian*. The bride wore a dress of white satin trimmed with silver and old Brussels lace. It was elegant, with a high neck, and just visible is the present from the groom of an amethyst and diamond necklace. There were cascading bouquets. Kate's husband, now the Reverend Rolly Sale, officiated. There followed an astonishing list of wedding presents. It was fashionable in those days to lay out the presents for inspection, with cards from the givers, and these included a Venetian glass vase from Mrs Arthur Bradshaw, which must be a mistake as this was seven years before Arthur was married. It was probably meant to be Mr Arthur Bradshaw. He acted as best man, and his sister Emma Louisa was a bridesmaid in a cream spotted net with a hat trimmed with violets. The album continues after the wedding, with holidays, the Steeple Aston Flower Show, family letters and watercolours by Doreen.

About Bob, who was tall and gangly with a long horse face, there is not much information. He was often photographed at The Grange, where he stared at the camera with the air of a lugubrious gangster, his hat pulled down over his eyes. Seldom photographed without a cap, he smoked a pipe and played golf and tennis. Before his marriage he went to the beach on family outings and took part in the activities at The Grange, always present at the annual flower show. He spent his working life at the brewery with John and Stewart. None of these men had children. Could something in the brewing industry have been responsible?

If information about Bob is sketchy, Harry could best be described as absent. In all fourteen albums there are only two photos of him, in uniform, on his return from the Boer War. He was reportedly adventurous, keen on cricket and hunting and he may have spent a few years after he left school at The Grange indulging in country pursuits. Then he set off for the goldfields of Witwatersrand and nothing more was heard of him until early 1900.

The two daughters, Katherine and Emma Louisa, were tutored at home with a governess, Alma Abbott, but Kate was resentful and very much wanted to go to school. Or leave home. But it wasn't until she was thirty that she married the Rev. Thomas Rawlinson Sale and moved to Lancashire where he had the parish of Leesfield. Rolly Sale, born 1865, went to school at Marlborough, followed by New College, Oxford, from where he graduated in 1884. He married Kate in 1897, the year before the photo albums came into being, so there sadly isn't a wedding picture. Indeed, there are very few photos of the two together. Thereafter it is mostly their children, Tom, Jack, Mary, and Elizabeth, who feature at The Grange.

Emma Louisa stayed at home at The Grange. Known in the family as Lil, she was a large, rather plain and placid looking woman, never without a bit of sewing on hand. She played the piano and painted a bit and had no marriage prospects, but children adored her; she was kind and loving and content just to be with her family.

In 1891 the youngest, Arthur, aged 12, was a boarder at Summertown school in St Giles's Parish, on the Banbury Road in Oxford. Before the parish was formed out of St Giles's, in 1834, there was a Sunday school, but the school no longer exists and, according to the Oxford Archives, nor do the records of attendance.

Two years later, in January, when Arthur turned fourteen and was set on following his father into the navy, he completed four years and three months of training, first on the *SS Britannia* and subsequently on the *SS Derwent*. In 1899 he qualified as Second Mate in the Merchant Marine and was issued with a Certificate of Competency, but he did not hold this post for long, owing to the lung problems which plagued him all his life. During his final voyage to Australia that year, his father died. Memories of his life in the navy faded over the years and the only legacies were a penchant for salty expressions and a rolling gait.

1899

Faint laughter from children playing out of sight, together with the smell of wood smoke from a cottage fire, drifted up to where Emma stood at the open window. It was very early. The sun not yet risen and the garden, pale and shadowy, was wreathed in fog, the damp air heavy with portents of thunder. Not today, said Emma silently, please not today.

Richard lay downstairs in the front room where flowers from the garden were arranged on every surface. His final illness had been lingering, a year of poor health but the end was mercifully short, and his funeral was to be at eleven o'clock at the church of St Peter and St Paul. Carriages had been ordered.

It was late June and there had been a thunderstorm almost every day for a week, though not until the afternoon, if she thought about it. Again, the laughter, punctuated by a shout. The laughter ceased abruptly and in the silence a bird began to sing. A skylark heralding the dawn.

This had been Richard's favourite view from their bedroom in the upper storey looking across the garden to where the trees, now in high summer and robed in full green, climbed the hill opposite the village.

Unable to bear the view in plain light, she turned from the window; wondering when she should go downstairs. The housemaids would be about, but still putting out the breakfast and she did not want to disrupt the routine, particularly as they would all be hurrying, needing to lay out the refreshments after church for the returning family and be on time for the funeral.

Someone, her old parlour maid perhaps, had placed the picture of Richard face down on her bureau, and his portrait was turned to face the wall. Emma did not believe in such superstitions and set the photograph upright. It was a good likeness, she thought.

At this moment a pain shot through her and she almost cried out. She had kept her grief to herself, maintaining an outwardly calm presence as she always had, knowing it was expected of her, but it had built inside and was becoming unendurable. Not today, she prayed, don't let me break down today.

She ran through the family in her mind, most of whom had already gathered at The Grange. Rolly and Kate were staying and offering great comfort and support. Rolly was assisting at the funeral so Kate would take care of her at the church and shield her from the more theatrical mourners. Some women in the village – but Emma checked herself, such uncharitable thoughts were not worthy of the occasion.

Stewart and Bob had arrived from the brewery, John and Mary Kathleen would be at the church and she would look after Emma Louisa, having more patience with her than her sister Kate, who was inclined to be impatient even with her own baby boy. The poor girl was distraught at her father's death and had little control over her emotions, being almost constantly in tears. Emma had thought it might be better if she didn't come to the funeral but there was no one to stay with her at The Grange. The house staff and the gardeners must all be allowed to come to the church.

Her son, Harry, was seeking his fortune in Africa where it was rumoured the Boers were gathering their forces for another war. She must write to let him know of his father's death. Tomorrow. And Arthur, her beloved youngest son was also at sea on what was to be his final voyage. He was sailing to Australia as third mate on the *Samar*.

This added to Emma's grief in a way that robbed her of sleep. If only Arthur had been at home. Emma put the thought aside.

There was a discreet tap on the door and her maid entered to help her dress. The bombazine was laid out ready; she would be garbed in black today, and every day for the rest of her life. Neither woman spoke much beyond the good morning courtesies, and Emma stood while she was laced into her bodice and petticoat and dress then helped with her stockings and shoes.

But when the maid lifted the silk bonnet with long crepe streamers, Emma reached out a hand to stay her. "I'll put that on later, when we leave for the church." The woman nodded and, leaving the bonnet aside on the dressing table, she edged from the room, closing the door quietly behind her.

Emma rose and went to the window again, forcing herself to look. Now the sun was up, the morning air was filled with the sounds of birds and voices and it was the most normal view in the world. She sighed deeply and, suddenly inexplicably ravenous, she reached for her handkerchief and turned to the door. She started slowly down the stairs to face the day.

The funeral was held according to Richard's wishes. In the words of the local paper, as in life, so in death, "the gallant officer had requested a service of an unpretentious nature" with just two hymns: Abide with Me and the Navy Hymn. Reference was made to his naval service, his actions, particularly during the Zulu Wars, his Order of the Bath, and his community spirit. Councillors, his colleagues on the bench and local school children mixed with the good folk of Steeple Aston and servants from The Grange. The Union Jack, which by virtue of his naval rank Richard was permitted to fly on the roof of the house, had been lowered to half-mast. His coffin was carried by his three sons, the chauffeur, and the gardeners from The Grange, and he was laid to rest under a tree a short distance from the west door of the church.

In the evening Emma stood again at the window, looking across the garden. It was late, the sun had almost set, the guests had gone and mercifully, following a short burst of thunder, so had the humidity. The flag had been lowered at sunset, folded by John and Stewart and put away.

Now released from her heavy bombazine, Emma breathed in the pure rain-washed air and felt it flow around her. Then she lifted her nightgown and let it cool her feet.

The family had dispersed, though Kate and Rolly had stayed on, and John and his wife would not return home till the weekend. The day had gone well. She had been the centre of attention, and people had been kind and generous in their praise of Richard, telling her things she already knew about her husband as though they were intimate revelations they must share. She smiled at this. Did they think it brought comfort, or was it just convention? No matter, it was done now. Emma Louisa had been put to bed after a light supper, without protest.

She pulled a chair closer to the window and was about to sit, when it seemed to her that she should stay standing in homage to Richard and his favourite view. How silly, she thought, as if he would know. But she stayed on her feet at the window watching the sun go down, and the long, long twilight start to change the shapes and colours of the garden, withdrawing the luminescence that she had seen lighten the view in the morning and replacing it with something different. How odd, she mused. Would you not expect that the light would come and go the same way?

She became aware of faint strains of music coming from below. Schubert. How appropriate. It must be Kathleen playing the piano. Mary Kathleen was John's wife and a talented pianist. Emma had known her all her life and loved her dearly. Emma listened, wishing she could hear more clearly, then suddenly somebody opened a window in the parlour and the music rose up to her as clear as the stream it described. Tears came, finally, and she sat down without thinking and gave way, as Mary finished the Schubert and started a Chopin nocturne. Emma felt a rush of relief followed by gratitude at her first real feelings of the day.

She sat watching as the twilight subtly faded the familiar landmarks and the dusk settled. Twilight, Emma thought. Lovely word, and it had a meaning – twixt or between light, or even a third light perhaps? Twilight was more than dusk, but today she wanted a word that meant more than twilight. Something to mark the end of *this* day and the passing of a life. And it came to her: endlight. Yes, she thought, endlight. That fits perfectly. And Emma sat until the night was properly dark and she could no longer see a single object in the garden. The music had long since faded, and all other sounds had ceased.

She rose stiffly and turned away from the window, leaving it open to the night air. An owl hooted. Endlight.

1900

Arthur returned from Australia in the February following his father's death. He brought a lyre bird's tail feathers as a present for his mother.

What is it like? the family asked.

"Different," said Arthur, "extremely hot and truly clear, deep blue skies. The people are friendly and mostly relaxed, though I went to a dance where the formality was of the white gloves variety, keeping up the traditions, and they think of England as Home."

Arthur went to the churchyard and stood by Richard's grave for a long time, thinking about his father and listening to the wind rustling in the big elms. Richard could not have known he was leaving the navy at the end of his voyage to Australia. Indeed, he hadn't been certain of it himself, and now he was glad his father had died without that knowledge as he would have been deeply disappointed. Arthur too, was disappointed but as things were turning out, even if his health had been able to stand up to the rigours of life at sea, there was the matter of who would take over managing The Grange. Emma was more than capable of running the household and the farm, but not in the long term, and with the older brothers already ensconced in their positions at the brewery and no suggestion that Harry might return home and assume the responsibility, it was down to him.

Leaving the church yard, Arthur found his mother waiting at the steps.

"I thought I'd walk home with you," she said.

Arthur smiled and put his arm around her. "Father has a nice resting place."

"I plan to lie beside him when the time comes."

"That won't be for many years, I hope."

"I am thinking of giving something to the church in your father's memory, perhaps a lectern?"

"An excellent idea. I am sure it will be greatly appreciated."

"Something simple, a polished timber ship's wheel with naval symbols for his various campaigns."

Arthur nodded. "Yes, that sounds appropriate."

"He was a good man, modest in his tastes, and he served this country well. He deserves to be remembered."

They crossed the road and entered the gates of The Grange.

"Let's walk a while in the garden," said Emma. After a little silence, she said "Is something troubling you, apart from you not being here when he died?"

Arthur halted, and gazed towards the woodland then took a deep breath and turned to face his mother. "I let him down," he said, "and I let myself down. I failed in the navy. I know he had expectations that I would follow in his footsteps and he would have been bitterly disappointed by my early departure. It looks like giving up."

Emma had been expecting this. "No," she said firmly. "You are not to think like that. I won't have it. Richard was very proud of you and yes, he hoped that you, the only son to follow him into the Navy, would have a brilliant career, but he of all people would have understood that your health, not you, was the cause of you leaving. God inflicted weak lungs upon you, my son. That is your lot. Now the navy's loss is my gain. To have you home to help me run this place is a wish fulfilled."

"But I don't know anything about running an estate," Arthur protested. "I have no experience of anything beyond a disciplined seafaring life."

Emma took his arm and they resumed their walk. "It's mostly common sense, and the discipline will stand you in good stead whatever you do. Everything for the running of this estate is in place as Richard had almost twenty years to set it up, and all the staff are loyal to the family and will assist to their utmost, you'll see. Besides, I know most of it and you can learn from me. You were lucky, you know."

Arthur was surprised. "What do you mean?"

"You saw more of your father than any of the other boys. You were only three when he retired and we came to live here, so you and Lil and Kate had his almost undivided attention until you went off to school. Harry was already at boarding school and the older boys were just leaving school and heading to the brewery."

"I remember he used to tell me stories about his African trophies that hang in the hall," said Arthur. "Sometimes he'd take down a spear and let me hold it for a minute. That was very exciting."

"And he always held your hand when you were little and we walked to church," said his mother, "he would lead you down the aisle to our family pew and you behaved so well during the service. When you were older it was different and there was a certain amount of pinching, which he frowned upon."

"Kate started that."

"I expect she did, Kate was easily bored."

"Do we still go to church every Sunday and sit in the same pew?"

"Yes, of course. It's our allotted place and we must set an example. The village expects it of us."

"So, Dad was regarded as the Squire because he lived in The Grange?"

"Indeed he was, and now it is your turn."

Inwardly, Arthur rolled his eyes. He knew he had responsibilities, but he had not bargained for the religious aspects of his role. However, he also knew this was not the time to express any misgivings to his mother. They rounded the corner of the house and looked towards the field where dairy cows were bunched at the gate, waiting to be milked.

"I know Lil and Kate didn't go to school," he said, "but what did they do?"

"Lil was happy with the farm, she had piano lessons and she had her sewing – she was a contented soul. Kate was a different matter. She always had a great deal of energy and she fretted because she wasn't allowed to go away to school, so she taught herself through reading, and she helped me about the house and garden. She also persuaded cook to teach her and for a while the house was full of the smell of her baking – delicious apple pies, sponges, biscuits, even bread. She generally kept busy until she met Rolly Sale."

"When was that?"

"He came down from Oxford in '91 with a master's degree and was appointed to the Bishop of Man as his domestic chaplain, I think. He and Kate met at Christmas the year after, and they would have got married sooner but Rolly had to have a decent living before he could afford a wife."

Emma paused, feeling something tickling her hair, and reached up. Arthur leaned over and removed a bee. She smiled her thanks. "When he had his own parish, they were married here, and I've never seen Kate so happy. She practically bolted down the aisle and Dad had to trot to keep up with her, so keen was she to marry Rolly. You missed the wedding as you were already in the navy."

"I hardly know him, but he seems a good man."

"Oh yes," said his mother, turning towards the house, "he is a very good man. Your father was much in favour and hoped that he might get this parish, but it was not to be. Now there are two grandsons and, bless Rolly, he and Kate visit frequently. Tom and Jack are sometimes left with me and they are dear, happy little boys."

Arthur knew that his mother longed for a tribe of grandchildren, but he felt this was not the moment to mention that John and Mary Kathleen had so far failed to produce an heir. Bob and Stewart were yet to marry, and he was unable to contemplate his own marriage, so there were still plenty of possibilities.

He turned with her and looked at the house, lit from within. To Emma there was still the magic she had felt on first sighting. "I love this house," she said.

Arthur nodded. "So do I."

At the start of the second Boer War in 1899 Harry, in Africa and always looking for adventure, had volunteered for The King's Own Rifles. This regiment, along with others, was under the command of Lieutenant General Sir George White, a distinguished but elderly soldier. Unfortunately, the warfare in the Natal was beyond his experience and capability, and although he knew he should not allow his troops to be pinned down in the minor township of Ladysmith, instead of retreating he stayed, as he could not bring himself to abandon the stockpile of army supplies built up in the township.

On 2nd November, the railway line to the south was cut, and the siege of Ladysmith began. The British were overconfident and underprepared for the conflict. Harry wrote to his mother during the siege, a long, and in parts harrowing, letter. He described the artillery bombardments, the boredom when there was no fighting, the death of friends, the lack of supplies and the shooting of cavalry horses for food, and above all, the lack of water. The relief by General Buller, when it finally came, was almost an anticlimax.

Nothing is known of Harry's circumstances before he joined up, but according to family sources, he was *"carried out of the Siege on the Butler's shoulders."* He must have been living well to have gone off to war with a butler.

Harry returned to The Grange to recuperate, but the pull of Africa was stronger than the pleasant, if unexciting, life in rural England. After reconnecting with friends, he spent a season hunting with the Bicester and Christmas with the family. Then he left again, this time for West Africa and more prospecting.

Arthur took an apartment in Marylebone, a stone's throw from the Wallace Collection, and spent much of his time in London enjoying an extended social interlude. Having been for most of his life either at boarding school or in the navy, for the first time he was free from institutions and could make his own friends. At the suggestion of his brother, John, that he broaden his acquaintance by joining a Masonic Lodge, in 1903 he joined the Clapton, the first of many.

It was the early days of the sporting King Edward VII's brief reign with his beautiful Queen Alexandra, and a lighter atmosphere pervaded society. London was a great place to be; gone was the mourning black, the stuffy gloom, the aspidistras, and the antimacassars of the Victorian era. It was not far to visit his aunt Emily and her three daughters in South Kensington, or to Arnos Grove to visit the Walker cricketing cousins. His brothers, except for Harry, were all employed at the brewery so he could look in on them at the Barley Mow brewery at Limehouse on the Thames. He may have toyed with the idea of joining them, but The Grange had fallen to his lot. His father had left the estate in good condition, but it had to be maintained. Richard had left very little money, less than two thousand pounds, and that to Emma and his brother John, so the brewery provided for the upkeep.

At twenty, Arthur was six feet tall, good looking and fair, with blue eyes. He wore his brown hair parted with razor sharpness in the middle. He was described by a friend as "radiating happiness and charm" but his family added that on occasion, he had a volcanic temper. He was very gregarious and enjoyed travelling; when it was necessary to add his profession to a passenger list, he described himself as "a gentleman". His nickname in the family was Moses, shortened to

Mo. Nobody knew how he came by it, though there is a look of an Old Testament prophet about him in some photos. His sister, Emma Louise, was nicknamed Lil, to distinguish her from her mother Emma. This was a family that bestowed diminutives upon their members.

Christmas 1903 at The Grange, the whole family gathered, offering Arthur advice on how to run the estate, the staff and the house that had fallen to his inheritance. Emma was ready to step back from full responsibility. The estate, comprising twenty-eight acres, had a farm, a dairy and several cottages. At full strength there was a staff of eighteen: the butler Charlie Hart, a footman, chauffeur Will Butler, head gardener Dick Wadham and six under-gardeners, Tommy Nelson the cowman, Cook, Nancy the kitchen maid, the head housemaid and three under-housemaids, and a "boots" who cleaned cutlery and did odd jobs.

Even with fires in the main rooms, upstairs the house was freezing, and over Christmas Arthur's bronchitis progressively worsened until he took to his bed.

Perhaps you should give up London and get away for the winter, suggested Kate, always practical. But where to go?

"Father always spoke admiringly of the climate in southern Africa and the beauty of Cape Town," said Kate. "Harry is somewhere out there, and we have a cousin, Hugh, in the army and lately married. Shall I write to him?"

And so it was that Arthur, armed with letters of introduction and an invitation to spend Christmas with Hugh and Adeline Bradshaw in Alliwal North on the Cape, sailed the following October. He would be away for almost five months and it set a pattern he followed most winters for the next nine years.

The time Arthur spent in South Africa which, according to family reports was considerable, is a mystery. Apart from a few sentences in a book about the Olympic Sports Club, of which Arthur was a member and a generous donor, there is no record. He supposedly wintered there frequently to get away from the cold in England which affected his lungs so badly, but the shipping annals and passenger lists are patchy, and he left no records, no letters or post cards. An obituary in the Cape Times suggests he was "resident" in Cape Town between 1905 and 1914, however there are photos of him playing golf in Cornwall in 1907 and there is a shipping record of his return to England in 1912, the year following his mother's death. He was also present at the Steeple Aston Flower Show in September 1913, so it is clear that he came and went.

The Cape Town where Arthur arrived in the early 1900s was a very different city from that visited by his father in 1873 when, as Captain of *HMS Encounter*, he had provided a naval brigade for the now largely forgotten Ashanti war. Cape Town in the 1870s had a population of barely 33,000, the railway station was still to be built and the first newspaper was not yet in print. Nevertheless, Richard Bradshaw was captivated by the dramatic and beautiful scenery and the mild climate. This favourable impression was reinforced when he diverted his ship *HMS Shah* to South Africa in 1878 to attend to the disaster of the Zulu War retreat of British soldiers across the Buffalo River. For his gallantry during that incident he received the praise of Parliament and made a Companion of the Order of the Bath.

In the 1870s the discovery of diamonds and gold in the Transvaal had led to great changes and although Johannesburg had increased in influence due to proximity to the goldfields, Cape Town as the principal port benefited from an increase in trade. When Arthur arrived, Cape Town was the capital of the Union of South Africa and the population in 1910 had grown to 200,000. There was a university and a botanical garden. However, political and economic power was now vested a thousand miles to the north in the Transvaal.

Following the South African war of 1899 an influx of refugees to Cape Town created more slum areas. After an outbreak of plague in 1901, concern for public health created the climate for municipal officers to enforce racial segregation, and the first townships were developed to "contain" disease and disorder.

Arriving as a visitor, Arthur probably would have been unaware of much of this and, with his letters of introduction, could confine himself to a safe, comfortable bubble of white middle-class residents with regency townhouses and carriages. It is quite probable that he stayed at the stately Mount Nelson Hotel, opened in 1899 to welcome guests of the Union-Castle Shipping Line, under the same ownership. The Nellie, as it was known locally was, and is, a Cape Town institution, and the first hotel in South Africa with hot and cold running water. Famous guests over the years since have included Winston Churchill, Rudyard Kipling, and Sir Arthur Conan Doyle, who held a séance there in 1828. John Lennon and the Dalai Lama meditated, each in their own way, in the gardens, and Queen Elizabeth celebrated her 21st birthday in the hotel.

Family anecdotes tell of Arthur "staying with the Cullinan family" and there is a tale of handfuls of South African cut diamonds, brought back from these visits, some of which were made into family jewellery worn to this day. The original connection between Arthur and the Cullinans has not been made but there are two possibilities.

Following the discovery of the great diamond in 1905, Thomas Cullinan took his family – wife Annie and nine of his ten children – to England for three months where they set up in style, with nursemaids at Claridge's, and toured the Continent. Arthur at the time was twenty-six, single, handsome, and well connected, with a flat in London. He may have been thought suitable as an escort for the eldest Cullinan daughter, Winifred. Also, although evidence points to Arthur spending a fair amount of time in Cape Town taking part in the activities of the Olympic Sports Club and other golf clubs, the length of his visits to South Africa suggests he had the time, and doubtless the opportunity, to visit Johannesburg where the Cullinans lived. Thomas Cullinan was at one stage elected to the Parliament based in Cape Town, whence he frequently travelled, so encounters might well have taken place there. There is no evidence that he was ever a member of the Olympic Sports Club. Indeed, his interests were mining, farming, and his family rather than sporting activities. However, according to his daughter Loveday, Arthur did stay with the Cullinan family, and would have benefited from his association with them.

Thomas Cullinan was a towering figure in his world. According to his biographer Nigel Helme, as well as a miner, builder, parliamentarian, philanthropist, and a devoted family man, he was a patriot and a friend to both Generals Smuts and Botha. According to Helme, he was a hard worker... Honest, generous, and compassionate, he fought all his life for racial and political harmony and industrial expansion. He was ahead of his times too, in his love of nature. He carried seedlings in the boot of his car which he would plant when he saw a needy spot. He also used the birch on his children, then apologised for beating them. Autres temps, autres mœurs.

A paragon it would seem, and an example to Arthur, but his name lives on only attached to a diamond. At that time, the biggest blue-white gem quality diamond ever found at 3,106 carats, the Cullinan diamond, was bought by the Transvaal government and presented to King Edward VII in 1907.

Arthur probably received a basic education in the appreciation of gemstones, and diamonds in particular, from Thomas Cullinan, touring his mine and sorting rooms and being instructed on the finer points. This may have awaked an aesthetic sense in Arthur that would develop over time and reach its full flowering when he encountered Fabergé in his later years.

The Olympic Sports Club, founded in 1904 in Rondebosch, Cape Town, was one of Arthur's favourite places. He felt most at home in the company of men; he was very much a club man, and the Olympic suited him perfectly, being composed entirely of amateur sportsmen who were gentlemen. He was nicknamed Braddie by the members. As at home with his memberships of the Steeple Aston Flower Show Committee, the Ancient Order of Foresters, and several Masonic lodges, these all-male preserves were a haven from the female-dominated world of The Grange.

The first mention of Arthur in the club minutes was at the special General Meeting in November 1911 when he seconded the motion to erect a squash court at the back of the Club at a cost not exceeding R 500.

In February 1912 an entertaining challenge for a cricket match was issued to the Olympic Sports Club by Johannes Goek, the local attorney for Krekeltjeddorp Cricket Club. Anxious to improve what he termed the already high standard of their local team, he suggested that the flower of Western Province cricket should meet them in friendly rivalry for a Saturday match. A wagon with eight oxen and a dozen watermelons would meet the train to convey the team to the ground. The Olympics were assured of a very fine playing area and requested to bring a new ball. Included for the purchase of said ball was the sum of 1s and 6d.

The challenge was accepted. On the appointed day the team boarded the train, but en route it was discovered that there were only ten players as the essential eleventh had cancelled at the last minute, owing to his mother's sudden illness. A plan had to be hastily concocted to overcome this oversight.

Arthur sat quietly on the train watching the landscape pass by and enjoyed several slices of watermelon on the ox-wagon. He was content with the day, happy to be amongst friends and in the warmth of a South African summer. He looked forward to playing cricket and was glad to go in to bat at whatever position was given to him. Far down the order, he hoped.

Reaching the ground, a stiff breeze was blowing. The local team won the toss and elected to bat; Arthur was sent to field at second slip and took a fine catch in the first over, but it was disallowed by the umpire. That set the tone for the game. After tea, Arthur went in to bat at number 9, the score at that stage was 8 for 121. He didn't last long, rapped on the pad by a swinging ball, there was a shout from the bowler and the umpire held up his finger. Arthur was out lbw for 13. Then a certain team member, heavily disguised, turned up to bat a second time at number 10, but a sharp puff of wind blew trousers against his famous legs and the Captain was unmasked. The wicket keeper put up his hand to stop the bowler. The Olympics lost by one run.

The following Easter nine members of the Olympic Sports Club, including Arthur, visited Kimberley for the South African Golf Championship and much was expected of them. Alas, the putting greens provided foreign playing conditions and four players were laid low with severe stomach upsets, so any hope of success rapidly faded.

It was not just the Olympic Sports Club where Arthur enjoyed membership and golf, then his favoured sport. He was a member of the Royal Cape Golf Club and the Western Province Golf Union. All three clubs were the beneficiaries of trophies given by him, and along with Messrs. A.B. Godbold and Francis Black, Arthur was also largely responsible for the formation of the South African Golf Union and acted as its honorary secretary for some years.

In 1914 he returned from South Africa in May, in time to marry the following month in Eastbourne, the week before war broke out.

Thereafter, there is no mention of Arthur in South Africa, nor any shipping record to indicate he visited the country again, for twenty-three years. However, he retained all his golf club memberships and stayed in touch with his South African friends, entertaining them on their visits to England.

1904

"I think the dining room should be moved upstairs," said Emma, "I'm sure it was meant to be there, but Richard felt it more convenient to have it downstairs next door to the kitchen. He was all for sparing the staff any extra work." The family were gathered for a birthday celebration for one of Kate and Rolly's little boys.

Stewart looked around the room. The lights were on in the middle of the day, but it was still slightly gloomy. However, they were all used to it. "Why now?" he said. "And where upstairs do you have in mind?"

"That long room directly above the kitchen that looks south, out into the garden," said Emma, "I think it would be a perfect place. Lots of light and a lovely view."

"It's a long way for staff to carry our food upstairs," said Kate, "and it will be cold by the time it gets there. It's just not practical, Mother, and I'm sure cook will hate the idea." Emma gave her daughter a sharp look. This was her idea, and this was her house, even if Arthur was now nominally the head of the family, but she said nothing.

"There is a device that could be installed that just lifts the food up from the kitchen," said Arthur. "There is one in my club in London and I think it is called a dumb waiter. It seems to work by pulling on a rope. It is like a large box with shelves and would only be needed for hot food so it wouldn't be too heavy."

There was a short silence while the family thought about moving the dining room. Then Stewart got up and walked to the kitchen, peered through the door, then made his way upstairs.

"Better go and see what he's doing," said Arthur, getting up from the table.

"Let us know," called Kate, who was staying put with the children who were waiting for their cake.

Upstairs in the room above the kitchen Steward was inspecting the corner that corresponded to the pantry beneath. "Mother is right," he said to Arthur. "This is a much nicer room, and there would be room for a small cupboard lift thing over here. It might work."

Arthur walked around the room. "It would be the butler's job to pull the waiter up from the kitchen," he said. "Hart might enjoy that. Besides, how much hot food do we actually have? There's breakfast; porridge, eggs, bacon, maybe another hot dish, and coffee. Lunch is usually a cold buffet with a hot dish in the winter, then for dinner: soup, the roast and vegetables, a cold sweet and cheese."

"That's quite a lot," said Stewart.

"Yes, but it doesn't all have to come up at once," said Arthur, "and breakfast is always laid out in advance in covered dishes. I think it is a good idea. I'm going to get the carpenter in to have a look. Then he'd better go to an establishment that's got one working and see how it's constructed."

"I bet you can buy one ready-made," said Stewart, who was often slightly ahead of the game, "just need a carpenter to install it."

At that moment Emma came into the room followed by the others. Arthur waved at the window. "Look how nice it is up here," he said. "This is an excellent idea, Mother. This is just an extra reception room, not used as much as the one next door which faces north and has the Adam fireplace. By my reckoning, this room is exactly the same size as the present dining room. I think we should move up." He turned to Emma, "What do you think? Should we move Dad's African souvenirs up here too?"

Emma didn't even have to think about that. "No," she said. "They must stay in the hall downstairs where he put them."

Arthur turned to his sister. "What do you think, Lil?"

It was the first time he had ever asked for her opinion. This was a big moment, and everyone was looking at her. Kate smiled encouragingly.

Lil took a deep breath. "I think this is a lovely room," she said, "and I would be happy if it were turned into the dining room providing it doesn't put Cook and the kitchen staff to too much trouble."

There was a little clapping, Emma nodded approvingly, and Lil blushed.

"That settles it," said Arthur. "My mother and sister think it's a good idea, so let's move up here. Stewart, you seem to know the ropes. Can you find out about the availability of a dumb waiter?"

While the rest of the family retreated downstairs to the dining room where cook was waiting to light the candles of the birthday cake, Lil lingered for a couple of minutes. Humming to herself she moved around the room imagining a change of colour on the walls and thinking that new curtains would be nice.

Although outwardly plain and unadorned, Lil's imagination was fuelled by reading illustrated magazines and her taste in furnishings secretly veered towards the luxurious, though in fact she had never decorated a room.

She looked up at the magnificent ceiling and imagined a chandelier, yellow for the walls, though brocade or paint? And the curtains in the same colour, though the same fabric might be too much. Velvet would be too heavy, so paint on the walls and brocade at the windows? What if they changed their minds and did decide to move all her father's African souvenirs up here to decorate the walls? And then the chairs might need some work when they were brought into the daylight. That could be expensive. What would her mother do? Emma was rich, and could do whatever she liked in the house, but she was also very conservative. Lil did not think she would approve of yellow silk and chandeliers.

She was saved from further dithering by Arthur appearing in the door. "Hurry up Lil," he said, smiling, "they are all waiting for you. It's birthday time. You can do up this room tomorrow."

1905

In Arthur's absence in the early years, the brothers and their respective wives arranged to spend Christmas with their mother or have her visit them. But Emma did not much like to travel in the winter. Although she returned often to her family home at Arnos Grove, she preferred to go in the warmer months. Arthur had returned in April 1905 to find Kate in a mood.

"You cannot leave mother alone for so long," she began. "Emma Louise is poor company. John and Stewart couldn't come at Christmas, their wives having laid other plans, so Rolly had to leave his church in the hands of a very young man so that we could come to be with her. So inconvenient. Christmas is our busiest time, as you know. I have been thinking. Perhaps it is time to arrange for a companion for mother. You should employ someone congenial to live in the house."

Arthur was aghast. "An outsider? The staff at The Grange have always come from the village. Do we not have a relative that can come?"

Kate gave him a look. "Perhaps," she said, "but how long might they stay? No, somebody paid is the answer. I shall place an advertisement in *The Lady*." Arthur looked puzzled. "It is an exceptionally genteel magazine," she continued, "where people can find domestic help. An educated woman, widowed perhaps, or unmarried and still at home with no prospects would be ideal." The thought fleetingly crossed her mind that Arthur himself might be a prospect and she determined to find someone plain and middle-aged.

Arthur still looked uncertain. "Would I have to pay a lot?"

"I don't think so," said Kate. "Most would be glad of a roof over their heads, away from their own families, and she would be fed and well treated. Mother is in reasonably good health, so really it is just a question of company, particularly during your long absences. Leave it with me. I shall write to *The Lady* and make enquiries."

And she did. Kate was small, like her mother, with the same round face but with contrasting sharp features, and very efficient. She moved briskly through life, getting things done, but with a compassionate streak as befitted a parson's wife. She was never too busy to listen to a parishioner's trials and tribulations.

Arthur left the matter of a companion for his mother entirely to his sister and before long there was a small batch of letters on the hall table from prospective applicants. Kate went through them carefully, assessing the handwriting, noting the age and circumstance of the writer, and their experience. Most she dismissed, particularly those who were very young or obviously elderly, or who expressed a desire to "live in the country". Finally, it was down to two candidates. Kate invited them to The Grange for an interview.

Emma, having been apprised of the possible arrangement, was very keen to take part, but Kate said, "No, I will meet the person first on my own, and if I think she is suitable she will be invited to take tea and meet you. It is better this way." Emma set her jaw. She wasn't used to having others make decisions for her, and Kate was being rather bossy about this. Though in theory Emma thought it might be a good idea.

On the appointed day the first applicant arrived to be met by three of Arthur's dogs at the front door, who set up barking. She drew her skirts around her and backed away, hovering on the top of the steps with half a mind to flee, but the butler opened the door, called off the dogs, took her name and ushered her into the parlour where Kate was waiting.

"Miss Glover," he announced, and closed the door. Kate looked at a pleasant looking middle-aged woman with a slightly pinched mouth and dark hair scraped into a neat bun. She was nervously twisting her hands.

Kate smiled. "Come and sit down, Miss Glover. Have you come far?"

Sarah Glover perched on the very edge of a chair. "From Durham," she said.

Kate consulted her letter. "You are widowed, I see. Have you held another position?"

"No," said Sarah. "I went home when my husband died, and I live with my elderly parents."

"How will they manage without you?"

"We are a large family and there are three other sisters in Durham who will be looking after Mum and Dad."

Kate nodded. She asked about Sarah's interests. Did she play card games, read, sew, play the piano, enjoy the garden? Apart from reading aloud there was little else that might be entertainment for Emma. It was heavy going, and Kate sighed, knowing within a few minutes that Sarah, though nicely presented, had no accomplishments. She was dull to such a degree that Kate rang for tea, made a few pleasant remarks about the weather and ushered her out without bothering to introduce her mother.

"What was wrong with her?" said Emma, who had caught a glimpse in the hall.

"Deadly dull," said Kate. "She didn't even play bezique."

"Oh well," said her mother, "that wouldn't have done." Bezique was Emma's favourite pastime and she was exceptionally good at it, as everyone in the family had found to their cost.

"Are there any more candidates?"

"Yes," said Kate, "there is another one tomorrow. Her name is Phillips and her father is a parson."

Violet Agnes Evelyn Phillips was a surprise. Kate contemplated the girl before her: plainly dressed, very tall and very thin, with a straight back, a long, horse face and overlarge chin, fine eyes, slightly unruly curly hair, and a calm demeanour. She was unperturbed by the dogs, bending to pat each in turn. She was also very young, just twenty-three, and while her youth was not quite what Kate had in mind, her letter said she had nursing experience. Looking at her, Kate had a good feeling.

"Please sit, Miss Phillips," she said, glancing at the list of names. "What do you like to be called?"

"Evelyn," said the girl softly.

Kate made a quick decision and rang the bell, ordered tea, and rose to leave the room. "Do you mind waiting here? I will fetch my mother."

"What is she like?" asked Emma.

"Very young," said Kate, "but there is something about her. I think you should meet her now, and we will find out together."

They entered the parlour and Evelyn rose immediately to her feet. Emma held out her hand. "Welcome to The Grange, Miss Phillips," she said. "Do you play bezique?"

A shadow of a smile flickered across the girl's face. "Yes, I do," she said. "My brother taught me when I was small."

There were two brothers it was discovered over tea. Her father, the Reverend Samuel Phillips, was a retired vicar from Monmouth and her mother, Mary Elizabeth, had a wonderful soprano voice and might have been an opera singer, but her father refused to allow her to go to Italy to train.

Kate noticed that Evelyn barely picked at a small cake. Manners probably, but no wonder she was so thin. The nursing experience seemed solid – a year and a half. It transpired that she had wanted to train as a doctor, but there was no money. But more than that, Emma appeared to like her despite the age difference. They talked in generalities. The girl was quite well educated, and Emma found herself nodding in agreement.

"My brother Arthur is the head of the house," Kate told Evelyn. "You will need his approval, but I think I can assure you of that. He goes abroad much of the time."

"When can you come?" said Emma.

Evelyn's parents brought her to The Grange the following week to be on trial for three months as Emma's companion. She had few possessions. Her father was an imposing figure, a very upright man over six feet tall, while her mother barely reached five feet, but she had an air about her; she too stood very straight and had abundant and beautiful hair. Kate gave them tea and, when they had gone, she left Evelyn to settle in. Arthur was at home when she arrived. He looked at the tall, thin girl with a long face, and he noticed that she bent to pat the dogs on arrival. That won her points with him. He agreed to take her on and she was soon absorbed into the household.

Evelyn became part of the family and acquired the nickname of Bet. She was very tall, five foot nine inches, and never weighed more than seven stone. So thin, they said, she could hide behind a lamp post. As with Arthur's familiar name, Moses, nobody could ever explain how Bet was derived from Violet Agnes Evelyn, but this is how she was known in the family for the rest of her life. It was a mysterious little circle of aliases, those who lived at The Grange: Mo, Bet and Lil.

Evelyn was tidying her room when there was a knock at the door. She opened it to find Emma with two baskets. "I want you to come with me," said Emma, "and I will show you around the garden."

She handed Emma one of the baskets, obliging her to put down the linen she'd been folding, and she followed Emma downstairs and out onto the lawn. "We'll go to the vegetables first," said Emma. "These are Dick Wadham's pride and joy and he wins prizes at the local show. Did you have a vegetable garden at home in Wales?"

"Yes," said Evelyn. "Father grew leeks and potatoes." They walked towards the south wall where the vegetables grew, passing the pond. A gaggle of geese rose as one from the grass at their approach and splashed into the pond, flapping and honking. Evelyn drew back in alarm. Emma hid her amusement. "They won't hurt you," she said. "They are tremendous watchdogs and have been used since Roman times as an early warning system against intruders."

Evelyn gazed at the big white birds. "Do you eat them?" she asked.

Emma considered her answer. "No," she said, "but their eggs are used in cooking. They are big, and rich, and Cook particularly likes them for cakes." She did not say that occasionally a goose, stuffed with apples, found its way onto the table at Christmas. It had been one of Richard's favourite dishes. However, mostly the cull was left to Dick, and it was understood that he shared the spoils with the staff.

Dick and two boys were forking over a patch of ground, digging up potatoes. The fresh earthy smell took Evelyn back to her father's small patch where she had helped as a child. Dick rose at the women's approach and rubbed his back. He wiped his hands on his trousers and touched his cap. "Morning, madam."

Emma smiled and nodded to the two lads who had straightened up. "I am showing Miss Phillips around the garden," she said. "I thought this would be a good place to start."

Dick nodded at Evelyn. "It's hard work," he said, waving at the four big beds, "but it supplies all we eat at The Grange. We're self-sufficient here, we are. And there's the greenhouse," he added, "where we grow tomatoes, cucumbers and cantaloupes." Evelyn had never heard of a cantaloupe. "Better than a pineapple if you ask me," said Dick. Evelyn had heard of pineapple but had never tasted one.

"We will have a pineapple when Arthur comes home from Africa," said Emma. "Cook can make a pineapple centrepiece with sherbet, from Mrs Beeton. It looks spectacular."

Evelyn wondered who Mrs Beeton was; her ignorance was beginning to overwhelm her, but she realised that there was much she could learn from Emma that would benefit her greatly if her situation were to change and she was obliged to find another position. Evelyn had no illusions; she was not beautiful, had no means nor any particular talent beyond her nursing training, and, though deeply romantic, she was pragmatic enough to know she had no marriage prospects in this social milieu. A future as a companion, or housekeeper would likely be her lot, so best that she learned all she could, now, from Emma as her instructor.

Leaving the gardeners to their toil, the two women made their way towards the flower gardens. Passing a large meadow Evelyn could see several horses grazing. "Do you ride?" asked Emma, realising too late that raised in a Welsh parsonage, her opportunities for riding would have been slim. But there were always pit ponies…

"No," said Evelyn, who regarded the horses with the same degree of suspicion she had accorded the geese.

"The boys can ride," said Emma. "Harry in particular hunts with great enthusiasm, and Arthur can ride too, but doesn't hunt." Evelyn couldn't think of anything to say. She noted that Kate and Emma Louisa hadn't been mentioned, and while she thought Kate, from brief acquaintance, capable of almost everything, she couldn't imagine Emma Louisa on a horse.

They could smell the roses before they saw them. A long trellis was foaming with pearly pink roses trained by Dick to ramble.

"Madame Alfred Carriere," said Emma, before Evelyn could ask. "An old rose but a lovely one, don't you think? Let's pick some to put in the drawing room." And she handed Evelyn a pair of secateurs and pointed out the flowers to cut. "Not the full-blown ones," she said.

"They won't last."

Their baskets full, the two women set off for the house. At the far edge of the driveway they could see Emma Louisa sitting on a stool, bent over with a sketchpad on her lap.

"What is she doing?" Evelyn asked.

"Drawing the house, I expect," said Emma, "Lil likes to paint in watercolours, but she always draws the subject first."

Emma Louisa looked up from under her hat and held her pencil at arm's length to measure the perspective. Evelyn knew she couldn't ask any more questions. This is not my world, she thought. This is so far from anything that I've known. How am I going to fit in here?

In the winter of 1907, the family proposed a holiday for Emma in the summer.

"Mother will be looking forward to this," said Arthur on his return from South Africa in May, "and I will join you for a week".

Living in rural landlocked Oxfordshire, the coast, and the sea in particular, drew them. Emma was always happy to go to a beach, so when Stewart suggested a trip to Cornwall, she jumped at the opportunity.

In June, escorted by Stewart and Clarie, Emma set off for St Ives. Almost as far south as they could go, they based themselves at the Tregenna Castle Hotel, a crenelated, granite building from 1784, facing the sea and softened by Virginia creeper. There were turkeys and white fantailed pigeons on the lawn, and Emma was immediately enchanted. They first visited Land's End, taking a great many photos mostly of the sea, including The Lizard peninsula, a sinister rock formation and a graveyard for shipping.

Clarie gazed at the remains of several wrecks and thought how wild and turbulent the sea looked even on a mild, sunny day. She shivered, thinking of the drowned sailors. She was a city girl born and bred and this was new to her.

Emma sensed her discomfort and touched her arm. "That's enough for today," she said, "Let's go and have tea."

Arthur joined them a week later to play golf with Stewart.

At breakfast, Emma said, "What shall we do today? We could play bezique. It's too windy to go out much and I don't expect you will play golf."

"Of course we will," said Arthur. "It is always windy at Lelant – part of the challenge of the course, Mama. Stewart and I will pay a round this morning, and after lunch we shall all go and find a sheltered village and do a bit of sightseeing."

"Mowzel is reasonably sheltered," said the lady behind the desk. "A tiny village with a walled harbour, very picturesque. Not far from here."

"That would be Mousehole?" asked Emma, remembering Cornish pronunciations could be quite different from the spellings. "Such a charming name."

"Pilchards," said Stewart suddenly. They all turned to look at him.

"What about pilchards?" said Arthur.

"There was a pilchard fishery at Mousehole for five hundred years," said Stewart, who would have been a trivia champion had there been such a person in 1907.

"Probably still smells of fish" said his wife, preparing to wrinkle her nose.

"There is still a fishing industry," said the lady behind the desk. "Mind, it keeps the village going. You will see the fleet in the harbour too, nice for photos," she said as she eyed the camera Clarie was holding.

"That's settled then," said Arthur. "Stewart and I will be off now, and will see you later, for lunch."

Emma wondered if she could divert the company later in the

day towards Newlyn, close by Mousehole and home to the famous Newlyn Art School. Emma was a great admirer of one of the leading lights, the painter Frederick Hall, and particularly watercolours of his charming, rustic Cornwall cottages. Perhaps she would find one for sale in Newlyn. Excitement seized her at the thought.

She wouldn't mind a walk, she thought, and wasn't put off by a brisk bit of wind; she just tied her bonnet on more firmly. Clarie might have to be coaxed out in the weather, though. Still a new bride, she was cosseted by Stewart, but she would do. A nice girl.

Over the next week, in fine if windy weather, Arthur and Stewart played golf in the morning within sight of the imposing St Uny's church. Stewart wondered aloud where the vicarage was as there didn't seem to be one.

"Buried under the sand," said one of the caddies. Arthur thought about that. The way the wind was blowing, it would be possible for them all to be buried under the sands if they stood still for long enough.

In the afternoons the family visited all five of the wide sandy beaches in the vicinity of St Ives. Porthmeor, facing the full force of the Atlantic, was the most dramatic.

"Keep moving," said Arthur.

In contrast, the clifftop walks later in the week, above Housel Bay where they were able to meander, were quite still when the wind had dropped.

They were accompanied by acquaintances from the hotel, a Mr and Mrs Capling who professed shared interests and were agreeable companions. Mr Capling had recognised Stewart as a fellow oarsman and member of the London Rowing Club, and it seemed natural to join forces.

Emma invited them to join their family for dinner and afterwards for a game of cards, which they did, not realising until too late that

Emma was a skilful and competitive bezique player against whom no one present could prevail. Emma had devised her own game which included four players and four short packs of cards. Stewart and Clarie retired early, so Arthur agreed to play Mrs Caplan while Emma took on her husband. It was no contest and the Bradshaws easily triumphed. The Caplan took it well, particularly as Mr Caplan had beaten Arthur by one hole on the golf course that morning.

"Are you all right, Mama? You seem a bit pensive." Arthur was helping Emma off with her coat on their return to the hotel after another beach excursion.

She smiled. "Yes, dear, I was just remembering the three years I spent at Torpoint with your father. Those were his last years in the navy. You were just a year old, so you won't remember anything, but it was a really happy time."

"Is it far from here? Perhaps we could go over for a day."

"I don't think so. Much as I'd love to, it is about sixty miles and we couldn't possibly make it there and back in a day. Anyway, it would not interest the others and it is sometimes a disappointment to visit places where one has been happy in one's youth. They are bound to have changed and they always seem so much smaller somehow. I'm just indulging myself – a moment of nostalgia – nothing to concern yourself about."

With that, Emma took her coat and turned towards the stairs. Arthur watched her go, wondering if he had been overly selfish spending every day on the golf course, and what could he do now to make his mother's holiday more enjoyable. He knew that her favourite place in the world was her childhood home of Arnos Grove. Though she visited it frequently, it had never diminished in either size or memory.

The other attraction of these home visits was his big brother John who lived nearby at Southgate with his lovely wife Mary Kathleen.

Emma had been waiting for years for grandchildren but there were none, and Arthur knew that bothered her. John was now chairman of the brewery, a tirelessly hard worker who, despite his elevated position, still took public transport. He was an exceptionally shy and retiring man who hardly every appeared at a public gathering but was deeply involved in local affairs, and quietly gave to each and every charitable appeal. He seldom came to Steeple Aston and even when he did, and Emma tried to arrange for a family photo on the steps of The Grange, he would politely refuse to be part of it.

Arthur wondered about this. There were all sorts in a family, he knew. At the other end of the spectrum was the adventurous, extrovert Harry, hardly ever at home but, he had heard, about to return from Africa. Then there was nervy Bob; kindly, cheerful, sporty Stewart, the racing man, and his delightful, droll, bossy sister Kate. Emma Louisa, although he knew her very well, was more difficult to categorise and Arthur did not spend time trying to analyse her; he had a vague feeling in the back of his mind that she would come into her own, probably when their mother died, God forbid!

He put that thought hastily aside and went in search of Stewart, who might have a positive suggestion, and a pint of ale for inspiration. He put the question about Harry's return to Stewart. "Have you heard that Harry is coming home?"

"I think he is already back."

"Why hasn't he been in touch then or appeared at The Grange?"

"Well, I've heard there is a girl."

"But he's been in Africa for years. How could he have met a girl?"

"Maybe he met her on his last visit home, and they kept in touch through letters," said Stewart mildly, knowing that Arthur never wrote to anyone.

Arthur decided to drop the subject and turned to his mother's entertainment.

"Cliff top walks seem to be the most popular with Mama," said Stewart. "Let's forgo the golf tomorrow and take a picnic lunch."

There was an easy walk along a ridge with magnificent views to the sea. The party ambled happily around St Ives and Penzance for some hours, then up to the spine of the hill where they ate their picnic, at one point looking down on the dramatic Carbis Bay Hotel, which prompted Arthur to return with Evelyn and Lil some years later, situated as it was, not far from his favourite Lelant Golf Club.

The following day they returned to Penzance at Arthur's request. "I saw an interesting house there," he said. "I'd like to take a closer look".

The grandly named Riviera Palace Hotel, a handsome building, offered luncheon, and as they waited for the soup, Arthur engaged the elderly waitress, a local, in conversation.

"Only just opened a year ago as a hotel," said she. "It was a private residence owned by the Bolitho family who were in banking; they *were* banking in Cornwall, and it was called Polwithin House. I worked there for a few years. Very nice people they were, but after Mr Bolitho died the bank was taken over and his widow sold the property."

There were similarities to The Grange, it was discovered during a walk after their excellent lunch, not least in the extensive and beautiful grounds surrounding the hotel, with manicured flower beds and fields dotted with grazing cows. A peaceful, pastoral scene thought Emma. "We must stay here next time," she said out loud, but they never did.

At the end of the war the hotel closed, and it became a Church of England high school for girls. Later it was renamed the St Clare School, and, finally, the wheel turned full circle and it became the Bolitho prep school until failure to attract enough pupils led to its final closure in 2017.

Left behind at The Grange with Emma Louisa, Evelyn wondered what she should do. It had been suggested that she visit her parents, but they were also travelling to visit her brother Branch, lately appointed to a living in the Lake District. Arthur was in London, so she roamed about the estate, exploring the woodland, talking to the gardeners, in particular Dick who took a liking to her and answered her questions, and patting the animals.

Lil watched her from the sunroom where she sat with her sewing. They had little in common and, more than once, she had wondered just what Evelyn was supposed to do for her mother that she didn't do. It had been explained that Evelyn had nursing experience, but her mother didn't appear to need nursing. She would have liked to make friends with Evelyn and knew she should make the first move but didn't know how. Evelyn did not seem interested in sewing or embroidery, she did not, so far as Lil knew, play the piano or paint in watercolours, so where to begin?

Arthur returned from London and breezed through the house. He noticed the two women sitting in silence but thought nothing of it. Collecting his golf clubs, he patted the dogs, waved, and set off to join his mother in Cornwall. And it would have continued like that, except that early one morning Emma Louisa heard singing and, looking out of the window, she saw Evelyn on the lawn, face turned to the sun, singing an old Welsh hymn. Lil knew the tune. She went quietly to the piano and played a few chords. The singing stopped almost immediately so she went quickly back to the window and called to Evelyn, "Please, do go on singing."

Evelyn turned, startled, and smiled nervously. "I didn't think anyone could hear me," she said.

"I could play for you, if you'd like to come into the sunroom," said Lil tentatively.

There was a pause, then Evelyn said, "Thank you, but perhaps another time," and, turning away, she walked off towards the woodland.

Lil leaned on the windowsill and watched her go, then she went back to the piano feeling happy that a connection had been made. She hoped it was the first step towards what might, properly nurtured, become a friendship.

Later in June the holiday continued for Emma, this time with Lil and Aunt Rosa at Tenby in Pembrokeshire. Stewart and Clarie had returned home to Whyteleafe and Arthur had business to attend to at The Grange. The ladies, with others unnamed, were photographed picnicking rather uncomfortably on a rocky slope. Some of the photos taken at this time are excellent, both in composition and clarity, which could suggest that Emma Louisa was the photographer. Who else was travelling with them is impossible to know as, apart from the picnic, there are no pictures of people, and the scenes are mostly of the sea, ships and the beach looking to St Catherine's Island.

One morning at the hotel they heard there was to be a demonstration of a Lifesaving Apparatus at a nearby beach. They hurried with the camera to find a contraption had been arranged facing the ocean, surrounded by a crowd of interested onlookers. This was the Rocket, whereby a mortar was fired carrying a line to a stricken ship, which was then used to pull a boat out to the ship and carry the crew back to shore. After the gun went off with a loud bang, issuing clouds of smoke much to the delight of several small boys who were watching on the outskirts of the crowd, a person, ostensibly drowned (even more exciting) was laid out on the beach and rolled on his side to expel the water.

Emma, who knew it was just a show, was all for leaving at that point, but Lil, for whom such things were quite real, was not convinced. "I want to see that he is not dead," she said, and so they waited until the man got up of his own accord and walked away.

On another occasion they happened upon strings of horses belonging to the Pembroke Yeomanry practising their manoeuvres on the sand. This regiment, formed during the French Revolutionary Wars, had seen service in the Boer War and would again be involved in World War I, but that is another story. They also visited and photographed the ruins of the once magnificent Carew Castle, and spent a day Lydstep Haven, with dramatic cliffs and a beautiful, sheltered lagoon beach. But Emma, by then, had had enough of travel.

In the evening she was looking out to sea when Emma Louisa joined her on the balcony. "Look at the sky, Mama."

Emma turned and saw the undulating lines of little fleecy clouds radiating up from the horizon like badly combed hair; low lit by an apricot sun. "How pretty," she said. "That is a mackerel sky and that means rain. Time to go home." As Emma Louisa started to protest, she said firmly, "Yes Lil, we must think about getting ready for the flower show."

At home, a wedding invitation was waiting for her. Harry was marrying Miss Agnes James the following month. In Devon. Unlike Arthur, his mother was not completely taken by surprise. She remembered Harry bringing Agnes to The Grange the last time he was home in 1902 and there had been something between them to Emma's way of thinking. I'd have liked a bit more warning, she thought. He might have let us know – although Harry, always carefree, laughed his way through life, living from day to day.

Marriage will change all that, thought Emma.

1908

The morning post brought a letter from John. Arthur put it aside, assuming it was some sort of brewery business, and left it on the table where Emma saw it later that afternoon.

"What does your brother want?" she asked.

"I don't know," said Arthur. Emma walked away, down the steps and into the garden. Arthur looked at the letter and sighed then, knowing his mother would continue to ask about it he opened it.

It wasn't business; it was bad news. Their brother Harry was gravely ill in a sanatorium in Gloucester and his wife, Agnes, had written in desperation to John. Harry had expressed his greatest wish, that after his death he was to be returned to Steeple Aston and buried in the family churchyard.

Arthur stood, somewhat shocked, with the letter in his hand, and thought for a while about Harry, eight years older than he but still the brother closest in age. He hardly knew this man – different school, different paths – but he had been something of a hero to Arthur. He had cut a dashing figure, an energetic and sporting chap, a keen huntsman - riding out with the Bicester, a cricketer and, romantically, he had gone out to South Africa to seek his fortune on the gold fields, though before Arthur's time in that part of the world.

The dogs, sensing a mood, had gathered quietly around his feet. He lit a cigarette, stumbled, trod on a dog who yelped, then went in search of his mother. Emma was sitting on her favourite garden seat, bathed in the late afternoon sun, eyes closed, hands folded in her lap, smiling. Arthur sat beside her and laid his hand on hers.

Neither spoke for a moment, then Arthur said, "It's Harry."

Emma's eyes flared. "What about Harry?" she said. "We've heard nothing for a while."

There was no gentle way of putting it. "His wife has written to John. Apparently, Harry is very ill and may be near death. He wants to be buried here."

Emma sat up. "Where is he?" she said. "We must go to him."

"He's in a sanatorium," said Arthur, "somewhere in Gloucestershire, a place called Cranham. I will send John a telegram and we will make a plan."

Emma rose stiffly from the garden seat and reached for her cane. "I shall walk over to see the vicar," she said.

Arthur watched her move slowly towards the road and looked again at the letter.

During the Boer War Harry had joined a colonial unit, the Border Mounted Rifles. Listed as Trooper 341, he had been at Ladysmith, and after The Relief, when the Boers retreated to Biggarsberg, had returned to The Grange for a spell. Arthur too had returned and had seen something of him, then he had gone back to West Africa presumably for more adventure. Gold perhaps? The Ivory Coast? Arthur didn't know.

John's letter regretted that they hadn't seen much of Harry recently. He and Agnes had married the year before, and they had remained in Devon to live near her family. Arthur had not attended the wedding, but Emma went, as did Stewart, John, and their wives. Harry had reportedly not seemed well, but he was clearly happy. A daughter had been born in July and now, unfairly, Harry was dying. But of what, and why at Cranham? It wasn't that far away by Arthur's reckoning. About fifty miles to the west. He could drive over. He knew his mother would want to come. I must grasp the nettle, Arthur said to himself. I will telegraph John.

Just then Emma's companion Evelyn, emerged from the side of the house, carrying a shawl for Emma against the evening chill.

"Hurry after her," said Arthur. "We've had bad news and Mother is off to the vicarage. Go with her if you will." She caught up with his mother, placed the shawl around her shoulders and carefully guided her through the gate. He watched the two women, one tall and thin, the other short and round, leaning into each other, then he turned and went into the house, squared his shoulders and reached for pen and paper, and wrote to John, suggesting he come to The Grange as soon as possible and they would drive over with Emma to visit Harry at Cranham. It was not far from Oxford.

Then he called a boy from the garden. "Take this as fast as you can to the telegraph office," he said. "You know where the bicycles are?" The boy nodded, took the message and ran.

John's reply was swift but added little to what he'd written. Cranham Lodge was a sanatorium for tuberculosis, the town of Cranham was surrounded by picturesque beech woods, and it was not that far from Oxford. He would come to The Grange tomorrow evening and go with Arthur and Emma to visit Harry. Depending on his state of health, the rest of the family could then be summoned.

The Cotswold sanatorium is now mostly remembered for one famous patient, George Orwell, who completed his novel *1984* while being treated there for advanced tuberculosis. It was set in a wooded area, with individual thatched cottages for patients. Arthur, Emma, and John found Harry in one of these, in a very bad way. His tuberculosis was far advanced and there was no hope of recovery. Agnes, collapsed with grief, had been given a bed in the same cottage but her baby daughter was being tended to by a nurse elsewhere to guard against infection. Harry clutched his mother's hands and turned his sunken eyes on his brothers.

"Take me home," he pleaded.

Arthur nodded. "That's what we've come to do old boy," he said. "Now you rest quiet and save your breath, John and I will make the arrangements."

"I think you should warn the family," said the doctor.

"He wants to come home," said John.

The doctor was blunt: Harry couldn't make the journey to Steeple Aston by car, and in his opinion the poor man had a day, two at most, to live.

"We will stay with him then," said Arthur.

"You will find comfortable lodgings in Painswick," said the doctor, "but please be prepared to be called at any hour."

Harry died at dusk on the following day, a mild, glimmering evening, with his two brothers, mother, wife and baby at his bedside. His body was returned to Steeple Aston where the rest of the family had gathered, and he was buried beside his father in the churchyard of St Peter and St Paul, as was his last wish. His obituary in the *Oxfordshire Weekly News* of 4th November 1908 listed his mourners, the sorrowing relatives, family, friends, the staff from The Grange, the numerous wreaths, and the hymns. His brother-in-law, The Rev Rolly Sale, assisted at the funeral.

Later that year, at Flower Show time, two of Kate and Rolly's children who were staying at the Grange came down with a quite severe illness, so The Grange was obliged to close the gardens for the first time in the history of the society. The Show was held instead in a field lent by Mr. Taylor of Brasenose Farm. Arthur gave a cup for a massed display of fruit, flowers and vegetables. Mrs. Wadham won the table decorations.

***

The first week in June 1911 saw the roses blooming in the gardens at

The Grange and Emma was showing them off as she entertained a local friend, Mrs Hemingway, to afternoon tea on the lawn.

"Lovely weather," said Mrs. Hemingway reaching for a second scone, just as Emma suddenly bent over, knocking the tea tray onto the lawn and clutched at her chest with a cry of pain.

"Help," shouted Mrs Hemingway, and people came running. Dick Wadham was first on the scene followed by Evelyn, who had just returned from Brighton, and the housekeeper. Together they carried Emma inside and laid her on a sofa while Dick ran for the doctor.

After he examined Emma, the doctor looked grave, pronounced a heart seizure, and suggested the family be summoned with all haste. Rolly and Kate were first to arrive, and the following day Emma rallied and wanted to get up, but Kate persuaded her to stay quietly in bed. "Bet and I will look after things," she said.

Stewart and Clarie, John and Mary Kathleen, and Bob and Doreen all arrived soon after. Arthur was en route to South Africa and the news would not reach him for some weeks. He did not return to England until July the following year. Emma Louisa was distraught; she sat with her mother day and night until persuaded to rest. She took to gazing out of the window as if expecting Arthur to return, sobbing quietly.

On the third day Emma took a turn for the worse and died. She was seventy-seven.

"Merciful," said Mary Kathleen, "to go suddenly and not linger."

No one disagreed. The funeral was held the following Tuesday and the entire village turned out, children lined the street leading to St Peter and St Paul. The village was gaily decorated with flags and bunting in preparation for the coronation of King George V and Queen Mary the following week, and the church was filled with flowers from The Grange and overflowing with family, friends, and the great and the good, for Emma was much loved as well as admired for her charity and philanthropy. The *Banbury Advertiser* mentioned her kindly disposition and reported that "there was nothing promoted in the interests of the village that Mrs Bradshaw did not actively support."

"A little clumsy but we know what it means," said Stewart.

Emma the Matriarch was laid to rest beside Richard in the churchyard.

Evelyn might have left The Grange after Emma died, but Arthur asked her to stay on to take care of the household matters when he was travelling or in Africa for extended periods. Her parents had moved to Brighton and she sometimes stayed with them.

There was no conventional courtship between Arthur and Evelyn, and in no sense was it a great romance. That would have been unsuitable given the circumstances. Emma, watchful in the beginning, had soon come to the conclusion that Evelyn was virtuous and gave up worrying. Evelyn fell in love with Arthur early on and was clever in hiding her feelings from him, and from everyone else, all except Dick Wadham who had watched the two of them.

Dick had a theory that, just like the garden, people had their seasons. Arthur was in his springtime and he was enjoying every moment. That was as it should be. All those girls who came from London with their pretty dresses for the big house parties, for Ascot and Henley, they were all very well but would likely fade by the end of summer. Now Miss Evelyn, as he called her, she would last through winter. He just hoped Arthur could see what was under his nose.

Arthur simply got used to Evelyn being there. He discovered that when she was away, he missed her and thought more and more about her on the long voyages to and from Africa.

Arthur was no innocent. His years in the navy had introduced him to ladies of the dockside, there had been a cheerful blond tennis player with whom he flirted in South Africa, and back in London, the debutante daughter of an earl had entertained him in her spare time.

Evelyn, however, was a different matter. Two years after his mother's death he was now well aware that she was in love with him. And she loved the dogs. More, she loved The Grange and in due course was able to run the house, much as Emma had done, from years of absorbing her elderly employer's methods and routines. Emma had been kind to everyone, particularly those who worked for her, and Evelyn had no trouble in following in that vein.

She had no other man ever in her life, and her closest friend was Eileen Rutledge, known in the family as Ailey, with whom she had done her nursing training and who was now a matron. They wrote to each other every day and Ailey was a frequent visitor to The Grange in later years, often going on holiday with the family. She was a practical, forthright woman, and a guest was once somewhat surprised at hearing Ailey voice her not very flattering opinion about a local dignitary at a lunch party. He said as much to Arthur who, devoted as he was to his wife's best friend, knew that she could be abrasive. "Ailey?" he said. "Yes, she can be a bit too honest. I'd say that if you want to know your shortcomings you won't find a more helpful person, anywhere."

In 1913, as Arthur was preparing for his African sojourn, he had a sudden premonition that Evelyn might not be at home when he returned. He was struck with the realisation that he was extremely fond of her and felt slightly panic-stricken. Accompanied by two dogs, he went to find her in the garden where she was snipping bits off a vine. She too, was distressed at the thought of his being away again for a long time.

Arthur stood and watched her for a while. If she was aware of his presence, she gave no sign. He saw how the sunlight caught her hair and he thought how soft it looked. He wondered if it would feel soft to the touch, then checked himself and returned to the house without speaking.

He spent the night before he sailed sleepless, wondering what to do. Family lore has it that she went to the station to see him off, and as the train was pulling out, he rolled down the window, tossed her his signet ring, and over the shrieking whistles and billowing steam, shouted: "Will you marry me?" She smiled, waved and he took that as a yes, which of course it was.

She did not see him for another six months. Evelyn wore his signet ring, which eventually was passed on to her daughter Loveday. One would like to think that Arthur returned from that trip in 1914 with a huge, sparkling diamond, but there is no record of such a ring. Diamonds there certainly were, and some have trickled down as family heirlooms, but what became of most of them, and the magnificent pearl that Evelyn wore for her formal portrait photograph, is not known.

1914

Arthur and Evelyn were married on 17th June 1914 at St Saviour's Eastbourne, witnessed by Arthur's brother Richard and A.H. Tregidga. He was thirty-five and she was thirty-two. Evelyn's address was given as Park View, Eastbourne. It was a morning wedding. There is a photo of them standing on the carpeted steps of what seems to be a hotel; he is smiling, she is solemn, but more, she looks as though she can hardly believe what has happened.

Evelyn wore a long-sleeved, slim fitting white dress with a matching feather boa, a black hat adorned with ruffles and flowers chosen by her mother, and she carried a trailing bouquet of mixed flowers and maidenhair fern tied with long floral ribbons. Arthur wore a dark three-piece suit, a pearl stick pin, a buttonhole of jasmine, patent leather shoes and would have been a picture of sartorial splendour but for the straw boater, a nod to summer but far too small for his head. He carried gloves and, for once, was without a cigarette.

"Happy?" said Arthur, as they waited for the photographer who was fiddling with his camera.

Evelyn looked at him, speechless. She'd had six months while he was away to dream about this day, and now it was finally here she felt numb.

Ailey had warned her. "I know you," she said to her friend, "you build things up inside you, you will plan what to wear and anticipate feeling a great burst of happiness, but it may not be like that. Don't worry, it will come but perhaps not on The Day."

Arthur took Evelyn to London for a week. They stayed at The Savoy with a view of the Thames, attended a musical theatre to see *The Belle of New York*, and visited the Walker cousins at Arnos Grove. He took her to Selfridge's for some smart clothes where she was so intimidated by the superior women in that department that, on their first excursion, she left with nothing.

Arthur contacted his aunt Emily who lived in Kensington, and she agreed to accompany them on their return visit. Emily brought her friend, Baroness Margaret Halkett, who had three fashionable daughters and an imperious manner.

She looked at Evelyn. "Lucky girl," she said enviously, "to be so slim."

Arthur explained they lived in the country, but would be attending Ascot, Henley and possibly Hunt balls. The Baroness then requested models to show a suitable wardrobe for these country pursuits, and at the end of an exhausting day, when Evelyn had her tweeds, evening dresses and smart summer outfits, Emily turned to Evelyn and Arthur. "That was a most entertaining day. Now you must let us treat you to champagne at Claridges."

Eleven days later a shot rang out in Sarajevo, heralding the war that would change the world forever.

"We have an invitation to luncheon with some people called Lacey," Evelyn said, passing a letter across to Arthur at the breakfast table. "Who are they?"

"Friends of my parents", he replied, "or rather their parents were. They always came to our flower show. I think these Laceys are our generation, perhaps a bit older."

"Don't you know them?"

"Not really. I have only met them once or twice. They seem nice and I gather they have a beautiful Queen Anne house on the other side of Oxford. We should go. I expect they want to inspect the new bride. Will you ring them up, or shall I?"

He saw Evelyn hesitate. "I'll do it," he said. He glanced at the invitation. "Leave it to me."

On the appointed day Evelyn dressed more carefully than usual.

"Sorry dogs," said Arthur, as Will brought the car to the front steps. "You can't come, not today." The tail wagging turned to disappointed drooping as the dachshunds sat and watched their master drive away.

The Laceys did indeed live in an original Queen Anne house, Roughley Hall circa 1710 with tall windows and a Palladian front, near Woodstock. There was a long drive bordered by stately trees and sweeping lawns. Evelyn's nervousness grew as she saw that several other cars had already pulled up and well-dressed people were alighting. "It's a big party," she breathed. Arthur took her hand.

"You look lovely," he said, "you needn't worry about a thing."

But he couldn't have been more wrong.

Brigadier Lacey and his wife were standing in the hall, receiving their guests. Their smiles widened as Arthur and Evelyn approached.

"Arthur Bradshaw!" Cecil Lacey exclaimed, "Good to see you, and is this your lovely bride?" He took Evelyn's hand. "My wife Isabel," he said turning her towards the pretty fair woman beside him in a silk dress and pearls.

Evelyn murmured something in greeting and moved away, further into the house, then she froze.

"What is it Bet?" Said Arthur. She had turned rather pale.

"I can't stay here, Mo," she whispered. "This house," she faltered, "this house is haunted by an evil spirit."

"Come on," said Arthur, trying to coax her into the drawing room where he could see other guests had gathered, one or two in uniform, and drinks were being handed round. A pair of springer spaniels lay in front of the fire and it looked nice, he thought, cosy, but I could do with a drink if she is going to be tricky. It's probably just nerves. "Come and meet some people."

"No," her voice rose. "I *must* leave here, Mo, now!"

"What's the problem?" The Brigadier arrived at Arthur's side. "Do come in my dear," and he took Evelyn's arm to steer her toward the door, but she rudely pulled away. "Is it the dogs? Are you frightened of 'em? I'll have them put outside."

"No, it's not the dogs," said Arthur, suddenly remembering something Evelyn's mother had said to him before they were married. He thought quickly. "I'm most awfully sorry, Lacey, I'm afraid my wife is not well, I do not think we can stay for lunch. In fact, I should take her home at once."

Cecil Lacey looked surprised and Arthur could tell he was about to insist when, to his great relief, Isabel, having heard part of the exchange, appeared at her husband's elbow, and sized up the situation in a flash. "Of course," she said, coming to the rescue. "If you think it best, I will make your excuses and we'll hope to see you another time." She smiled at Evelyn.

"Thank you," said Arthur, steering his distressed wife towards the door. Will was summoned, and they drove home. Evelyn, her eyes brimming with tears, and Arthur wondering what had really upset her so much.

"What was that all about?" said the Brigadier to Isabel. "Very odd behaviour, I hope Bradshaw hasn't made a mistake there, marrying such a highly strung girl." He had no patience with nervous people. His wife looked at him.

"She is probably pregnant," she said, "and now, dear, will you please carry on with our guests? I must see to rearranging the luncheon table."

When Evelyn had calmed down, Arthur asked her to try and explain what had caused her to react so violently to the house, but all she could say was that it was inhabited by 'a bad spirit.' Something awful had happened in that house and she didn't know how the Laceys could bear to live there. Arthur, though sceptical of spirits, was sufficiently intrigued to want to learn more of the history of the Hall.

The Bodleian was the place to go for information, and Arthur found a librarian who was genuinely interested in old houses and happy to look up Roughley Hall. A week later he received a phone call.

"Two murders," said the librarian succinctly, "and nasty ones."

Arthur felt a shiver. So, Evelyn had genuinely felt something in the house.

"A family living there in the 1780s had an only daughter who married a man who turned out to be violent and unpredictable," the librarian continued. "She ran away from him and returned to her parents, but the husband followed, broke into the house at night and strangled her, also killing their unborn child. Her parents heard screams and the father went to investigate, whereupon the husband set upon him too and bludgeoned him to death." The librarian paused.

"Did they catch the husband?"

"Oh yes, and he was tried and hanged. However, the poor mother was so grief-stricken she went mad and ended her days in an asylum. The Hall was empty after that for almost forty years."

Arthur thanked the librarian and put the phone down. It was a terrible story, a truly Gothic tragedy, and he felt a bit shaken. He wondered if he should tell Bet. He remembered that Lilla Phillips had told him Bet was fey, and this rather seemed to prove it. She had immediately sensed some horror in the house.

Would it confirm and allay her anxieties to tell her, he wondered, or make them worse?

He lit a cigarette and called the dogs. "Walks," he said, opening the door as the five dachshunds rushed past him down the steps. A good brisk walk in the woodland where the dogs could chase rabbits would give him time to think.

It fleetingly crossed his mind to wonder if Bet had ever heard the story about the ghost of an old General his mother had occasionally seen on the stairs. Bob claimed to have seen him too, once when he was very young, but Bob was inclined to be anxious and Arthur, who had never seen the General himself, discounted his story. He thought it best not to add to Bet's anxiety by mentioning a ghost just at this moment. Nor would he mention the tragedy at Roughley Hall in his letter of apology to the Laceys. To Arthur's way of thinking, sleeping dogs and ghost stories were best left undisturbed.

Evelyn's pregnancy was evident by October as her thin physique gave her away at four months. Emma Louisa was tremendously excited. She had been thrilled when Arthur and Evelyn were married, totally without rancour that Evelyn was displacing her as the Lady of the Manor, and she immediately started knitting.

At Christmas Kate, as a mother of four, offered some practical advice and baby clothes. However, Evelyn's mother Lilla, being the senior and having borne three children, wanted to take charge. Kate tactfully stepped aside but confided a few useful tips to Evelyn that were more up to date than those imparted by her mother.

Evelyn found that she had to sit down much of the time with this and subsequent pregnancies, and she wrote to tell Ailey who replied that she was concerned it was unhealthy; Evelyn needed fresh air, even in the winter. Arthur consulted Dick Wadham who knew someone in the village with a new wicker Bath chair they'd bought for an elderly relative who had died before it could be used. Arthur made an offer, and when it was gratefully accepted the Bath chair was wheeled along the road to The Grange where it became an essential prop and stay in Evelyn's life.

Lil, too, thought it was fun to ride on, but was discouraged by Arthur who, knowing Lil was a bit too heavy, said, "It's meant for

Bet. She needs it most of the time," and distracted his sister with suggestions of a picnic on the next fine day.

In February of the first year of the war, unable to get away to South Africa, Arthur took Evelyn, awaiting the birth of Loveday, and his sister Emma Louisa on holiday to the seaside resort of Carbis Bay in Cornwall. Arthur had spent the first few years of his life in Cornwall but had no memory of it, and, apart from the short holiday golfing with Stewart and his mother some years before, had not been back.

Adjacent to St Ives, Carbis Bay lies on the western coast of Cornwall, very near Land's End. They stayed in the Carbis Bay Hotel perched high on a hill overlooking the fine golden sandy beach. The hotel was built in 1894 by Cornwall's most famous architect of the nineteenth century, Sylvanus Travail, who was also responsible for several other hotels and the hospital of St Lawrence at Bodmin. It was an imposing, white painted, three-storeyed residence with forty-seven bedrooms in an elevated position facing the Celtic sea. Virginia Woolf stayed there in 1914 while recovering from one of her bouts of mental illness. She would later base her 1927 novel *To the Lighthouse* on the nearby Godrevy Lighthouse, and Rosamunde Pilcher featured the hotel (renamed The Sands) in her novels *The Shell Seekers* and *Winter Solstice*.

In spite of the fact that it was out of season and most of the young men on the staff – the shoe shine boy, and the lads who carried luggage up and down stairs and waited at tables – had gone off to join up and fight, the hotel maintained its standard of three excellent meals a day and a sumptuous high tea, Emma Louisa's favourite meal. There was only a handful of other guests: a young couple – she very pretty and he in uniform – obviously on their honeymoon, who gazed silently at each other and could be happened upon in the evening, clutched together in the shadows as if for the last time; and a family of four, the father with a pronounced limp and a patch over one eye, a wife with a serene expression and the auburn hair of a Botticelli angel, and two well behaved children.

A brief nod on entering the dining room was the preferred acknowledgement, but one day, after lunch, Arthur found himself in the garden with the father and offered him a cigarette. A conversation revealed that he'd sustained his injuries fighting in the Boer War.

"I had a brother there," said Arthur. "He died some time ago."

Mutual sympathy was expressed, then they returned to their respective families. The nods were more convivial thereafter, but it was a short-lived contact as one of their children developed a severe earache and the family left the hotel two days later.

For the Bradshaws, judging from the clothing, it was not a beach holiday, though undoubtedly the Cornwall weather was mild compared with Steeple Aston. They sat in deck chairs, the women wearing straw hats, Emma Louisa with her eternal sewing, Evelyn gazing into space and trying to gather her strength, and Arthur smoking, with a dachshund on his lap. They took in the sea air, taking it in turns to photograph each other.

Arthur, for whom idleness was no problem, walked with his dog on the beach; the dachshund liked the firm sand and scampered about, ears flapping, poking its nose into the flotsam of the tidal high water mark while Arthur looked up at the hotel and contemplated the life story of the architect.

Travail, he had read in a hotel brochure, had built seven hotels, four libraries, a grammar school, a technical school, St Catherine's Church, Mount Charles Chapel, and a hospital in Cornwall. He had been the Mayor of Truro and the President of the Society of Architects; a hugely successful career that brought him no happiness, for he had a history of depression and in 1903 he shot himself in the lavatory of a train; not far from Bodmin station.

Arthur found this story intriguing; a busy and productive life being seemingly no safeguard against misery suggested to him that it was not what one did, or did not do, that determined the state of one's mind, but who one intrinsically was.

He would have liked to visit all of Travail's hotels, always looking for ways of making The Grange, an unusual and in many ways inconvenient building, more liveable. The Headland Hotel at Newquay particularly attracted his attention, another grandiose building on a promontory facing the ocean. It seemed like just a day's journey, so he asked the manager to arrange for transport and lunch.

"We'll have a day out," he said to Evelyn. "Just us. Lil won't mind."

Arthur and Evelyn set off next morning, with the dog and a hamper, on the thirty-mile drive to visit the hotel. It was a bright sunny day, with a good breeze and woolly clouds. Cornwall was famous for its sunny days, and this was a perfect example. Evelyn wore a stylish outfit with a hat.

"You look so nice," said Arthur, taking her hand. She blushed; she still blushed when he said something like that. He was being tender with her. She smiled but said nothing.

The Headland had opened in 1900 after some stiff opposition from local fishermen who claimed it was on common land where they had dried their nets for generations. It was supposed to be a Victorian masterpiece, however the omnipresent Nikolaus Pevsner declared that, while it was certainly Victorian, it was "decidedly disappointing, and with no redeeming features."

Towering above Fistral beach, in 1911 the hotel welcomed both Edward, Prince of Wales and his brother Prince Albert, who had contracted measles and mumps respectively while at the Royal Naval College at Dartmouth. During World War II it served as an RAF hospital. In the future it would be the setting for filming a Roald Dahl story, *The Witches*. It has a Grade II listing, but apart from the position, it appears to be just a large, square, and rather ugly building.

Arthur found nothing in the way of new ideas, but the drive was pleasant. They spread their picnic lunch under a tree and admired the view, and on the way back, stopped off for tea at the seventeenth century St Agnes pub which, though without architectural merit, had a lively atmosphere. Returning to Carbis Bay they found Emma Louisa in the parlour. She beamed as they entered.

"Did you have a lovely day? I had a lovely day," she said. "The nice young couple asked me to have luncheon with them. He is from Falmouth. They have only been married for a week and he's off into the army next Monday!"

"How very kind," Evelyn murmured to the bride as they were leaving the dining room after supper.

The pretty girl smiled. "We didn't like to see her just sitting on her own," she said.

1915

Evelyn Loveday was born in April. The labour was long and slow, and Evelyn took time to recover. Too much time according to her friend Ailey. She should have been up and about, but instead was languishing in the Bath chair in the garden, trying to recuperate.

When Loveday, nicknamed Peggy, was two weeks old, Evelyn was photographed holding her, in her wicker chair, with her mother standing to one side, stiff with indignation as her authority had now been usurped by a prim nurse in close attendance, and Emma Louisa leaning down and staring intently at the baby. Everyone in the photo was projecting their emotions.

Arthur, who was standing a little apart with Ailey watching Kate take the photo, murmured, "The hand that rocks the cradle rules the world."

"Depends on whose hand," said Ailey, then, "Where did you hear that?"

"I can't remember," said Arthur, "I must have read it somewhere."

A week later, Loveday was photographed alone in Emma Louisa's arms, who was gazing at her with an expression approaching rapture. How she longed for a baby of her own.

Lilla, not to be outdone, insisted that the grandparents be photographed with the baby, albeit in a pram. The unspoken contest for control of Loveday went on until Eira was born two years later.

Loveday's proper name was established after a few weeks, but Evelyn just couldn't seem to get her strength back. Arthur was worried.

"I think she should see someone," said Matron Ailey. "A specialist. You will have to go to London."

Arthur didn't know any specialists.

"I will find out who best for her to see," said Ailey, and she made Evelyn an appointment with an esteemed Swiss doctor in Harley Street for early June.

Arthur and Evelyn were driven to London where they sat in an expensively decorated waiting room for half an hour, with a receptionist dressed as if she was off to a garden party, before a starched nurse appeared and led Evelyn away for her examination.

After a short time, Arthur was summoned. He found Evelyn sitting rigid and pale in the consulting room. The famous Dr Alphonse Gerber was ensconced behind an enormous desk decorated with a marble statue of a semi-nude lady and a gold carriage clock. He was dressed in a frock coat with a stiff collar; he wore steel rimmed spectacles, and had small soft white hands. Like slugs, Arthur said to himself. I wouldn't like him touching me. He rose to shake hands with Arthur then sat down again quickly. He steepled his fingers and gazed at a spot above Arthur's left ear.

"Mrs Bradshaw," he began. He cleared his throat. "Mrs Bradshaw has a rare and interesting condition."

Arthur stopped him. "Dr Gerber," he said, "my wife is here in the room. Kindly address your diagnosis to her."

The doctor's lips tightened, but he turned his gaze on Evelyn. "Mrs Bradshaw," he said softly, "you have *situs inversus*."

Arthur and Evelyn looked at each other. Dr Gerber smiled.

"Just what is that?" said Arthur.

"It means that your wife's major organs are reversed within her body. Her heart is on the right side, as are her stomach and spleen, while the liver and gall bladder are transposed to the left. The lungs are also transposed, along with nervous and lymphatic systems. It also means, I fear, Mrs Bradshaw, you will not be able to have children."

There was a short silence. Then Evelyn said, "I have a three-month-old daughter."

Dr Gerber went a little pink. "You didn't tell me that during my examination," he said, crossly.

"You didn't ask me any questions," Evelyn responded tartly. "You just listened to my heart, poked around a bit and asked if anything hurt, then made up your mind."

The consultation was concluded rapidly, and Evelyn and Arthur were bowed out of the consulting room and ushered quickly out of the waiting room by the smart receptionist.

In the car, uncharacteristically, Evelyn exploded: "He is a charlatan. He hardly examined me at all."

"I think," said Arthur, "once he determined that your heart was on the wrong side, he was so excited by discovering your rare and interesting condition he saw you not as a person but a disorder, and examined you no further.

"But does that explain why I have no energy and feel so weak and am sometimes in pain?"

"No," said Arthur, "I don't think so, but we must now find a doctor who can tell us, indeed help us to understand what this inverted condition actually means and if there is any treatment. And as for not having children, never heard anything so silly, what with little Loveday bouncing about, and I'm sure we will have more. Shall we go to tea at Claridge's? That will make us feel better. Then we can go and look at the new car I have ordered from America."

The new car was a black, two-seater Scripps Booth. A very rare bird indeed. Founded by James Scripps Booth, a self-taught artist and automotive designer, the eponymous company made cars from 1913 to 1923 at which time it was taken over by General Motors. The Scripps Booth joined a green Wolseley Limousine in the garage where it was lovingly tended by Will Butler. Arthur had bought this car immediately following his wedding the year before, but he did not drive. Evelyn only learned some time later, and she was still considered daring.

Situs inversus was first identified by Matthew Baillie, a British physician and pathologist, in 1790. It is an autosomal recessive disorder found in about one person in 10,000. In the most common cases it involves complete transposition of all the abdominal organs and affects all major structures within the thorax and abdomen, with most people having no medical symptoms or complications. Until the advent of modern medicine, it was usually undiagnosed. However, in up to 10% of people with the condition, there is a prevalence of congenital heart disease. This may have been Evelyn's problem, again undiagnosed, in consequence of her *situs inversus*. It would account for her lapses into tiredness and shortness of breath and the days, sometimes weeks, over the coming years when she had no energy and lay in her Bath chair, pushed around the garden by various family members when the weather was fine.

An autosomal (a chromosome that is not a sex chromosome) recessive disorder means two copies of an abnormal gene must be present for the disease or trait to develop. The parents of an individual with an autosomal recessive condition each carry one copy of the mutated gene, but they typically do not show signs and symptoms of the condition; it must therefore be assumed that both Evelyn's parents were carriers, but so far as we know, neither of her brothers were afflicted with *situs inversus*.

The war changed Oxford dramatically. Academic life virtually ceased, and many colleges had turned to housing wounded soldiers.

By August, Evelyn had recovered sufficiently to take part in a project that Arthur proposed after their return from Carbis Bay. "We should do something about a war effort," he said, "Let us have those soldiers that can, come over for tea, and they might enjoy a look around the garden too."

He consulted Dick who agreed that it would be possible to transport small groups around the grounds. And so it was arranged, and for several weeks groups of soldiers came to The Grange for a day's outing with a family. They were entertained by Evelyn and Emma Louisa to a lavish tea; Arthur offered a brief history of the house, and they were shown around the grounds, weather permitting.

A few of the married men, with babies at home who they were missing, asked if they could hold Loveday who was cooing in a pram in the garden. Evelyn would smile and lift the baby up and place her in the arms of a soldier. She was moved by the expressions of love on their faces. Good for both, no doubt, she said to herself.

The dogs also came in for lots of attention, and a game of bowls was on offer for those who were able, which added to the general enjoyment. In the evening, the soldiers returned to Oxford laden with food and flowers for their comrades who were too incapacitated to make the trip. If any of the soldiers wondered why Arthur was not in uniform, they kept it to themselves.

In 1915 the Flower Show was held as usual; the winner of the 'guess the weight of the iced cake' competition sent the cake to the Base Hospital for the wounded. A bowling match was held during the show between The Grange and the Banbury Conservative Club which was won by The Grange team. Arthur, Evelyn, and Emma Louisa, hosting the event, invited thirty wounded soldiers from Oxford. Proceeds were sent to the Banbury Red Cross.

Evelyn continued to suffer from indifferent health and there are a number of photos where she looks distinctly unwell, but whatever her ailment, it was episodic. When she felt well enough, she led a normal and very social life, dressing up to attend Royal Ascot, Henley, Hunt balls, and having large house parties to stay at The Grange. Boating on canals featured, as well the beach, fishing, camping, and hiking.

With her stick insect figure, the tailored post war fashions, particularly of the 20s and 30s suited her perfectly. Not one for frills at any time, her tweeds were well-cut, and the cloche hats contained her slightly unruly hair. She wore minimal jewellery, and apart from a riot of feather boa and flowers on her wedding day, the occasional floral fabric appeared only in midsummer at Henley. Her one great indulgence was perfume, the rich and extravagant Arpège that Arthur had given her on their honeymoon; he could sometimes find her simply by following the trail of scent she left behind her after descending the stairs.

Two more children were born: Kathleen Eira born March 1918 and Richard Edward, known as Bobby, in March 1921.

There were frequent visitors, often family members who might stay up to a month. In their old age, Evelyn's parents lived at The Grange, as did her close friend Eileen. Evelyn was, according to the family, completely impractical and had no sense of humour. But, following Emma's example, she apparently ran the household efficiently: breakfast was at 9 am, after which she would plan the day ahead, consulting cook about meals, and the head gardener about flowers for the house. She was fey as we know – in the Welsh tradition according to her children, and sensitive to the spirits, good or bad, in a house, and sometimes making predictions about the sex of an unborn child but not always getting it right.

She also kept secrets. Not long after her arrival at The Grange, she came down the grand staircase one evening and was passed by an elderly gentleman in uniform going up the stairs. She nodded in greeting, but he kept on going without acknowledgement. Odd, she thought, and rather rude. She told Emma when they were alone after dinner, who laid a hand on her arm and lowered her voice. "That was the ghost of the General. You were lucky to see him, very few ever do, but best not to mention it to anyone else. This is quite an old house, you know; built about two hundred years ago and the General was Prussian, as his uniform would seem bear out."

"Have you seen him?" Evelyn interrupted.

Emma smiled. "Yes" she said, "a few times, always and only on the staircase, but don't be alarmed. He is harmless, nothing violent happened here. He was a refugee from the Seven Years War, so the story goes." At this point Arthur came into the drawing room followed by his pack of dogs, and Emma never finished the story. Evelyn didn't tell anyone until she was old when she confided in her grandchildren.

A big part of life at The Grange was the annual Steeple Aston Flower and District Horticultural Show. The first recording of this event appears in Jackson's Oxford Journal of October 1862 as the charmingly named Steeple Aston Potatoe (sic) and Root Show. The following year the Potatoe was mercifully dropped and it became the Steeple Aston Root Show. Held in a field near Hill House Mansion, entertainment was provided by the Barton Brass Band and exhibits expanded beyond taters to include oranges and lemons. Over the next few years the show grew to embrace competitors from surrounded villages, and by 1868 there were "athletic sports for young men, racing by children and dancing on the turf." As well as potatoes, classes now included cabbages, celery, cobnuts, and flowers, particularly damask roses. The show went from strength to strength, and by 1874 two tents were required to hold all the exhibits. That year it was held in the grounds of The Grange, home of Captain Henry Bowyer. Gardens, model and cultivated, were included, and musical entertainment, now a feature of the show, was supplied by the Oxford Yeomanry Cavalry Band who played in the afternoon, followed by dancing in the evening.

From the early 1900s the show was held annually in the grounds of The Grange and was a highlight of the Steeple Aston year, held up as a shining example in the county uniting, as it did, six villages.

Arthur was usually the President of the Flower Show Committee and his friend George Child Villiers, the eighth Earl of Jersey, was the Patron. Villiers, for many years, had brought his gardeners T. Craddock and A. Perry, in charge at Middleton Park, to be judges of the horticultural section.

Emma, who loved her garden and was an expert artistic flower arranger, had extended her interest beyond Steeple Aston. At the Royal Oxfordshire Horticultural Society Commemoration Show in 1909 she entered several categories and was awarded first prizes for gloxinias, melons, cucumbers and tomatoes from the greenhouse, and a collection of produce from the large vegetable garden. Dick Wadham was properly given credit. Dick was also the secretary of the Flower Show committee from 1901 until his death. As far back as 1895 he was winning prizes in the Royal Oxfordshire Show for his chrysanthemums, Japanese anemones and fruit –strawberries, apples and pears.

The morning mail brought a letter from Kate.

"What does she say?" Emma Louisa was always avid for news of her sister. "Is she having another baby?"

Emma handed the letter across the table. "You read it, Lil." Emma Louisa took a bread and butter knife and slit the envelope with surgical precision while Emma watched. It sometimes amazed her that her daughter, a clumsy person to look at, could make such precise and meticulous gestures as well as delicate needlework and fine embroidery. She took out a short note, and a cutting from a Lancashire newspaper.

"Rolly has been appointed Vicar of Blackburn," she read. "The local paper welcomes the appointment; he has impeccable credentials, his services are spiritually earnest and musically bright, and he is possessed of a zeal for Christian work."

"All true," said Emma. "I hope this means a more comfortable living, and a bit more money. What does Kate say?"

Emma Louisa consulted her sister's letter. "They are delighted, the new vicarage has a big garden for the children to play in and Rolly is humbled by the appointment. Do you think he might be a bishop one day?"

Emma reached for the marmalade, noticing it was not home made and made a mental note to speak to Cook, while she thought about it. "No," she said slowly. "I don't think he is ambitious in that regard; I think he would prefer to remain in the parish, not set apart in the ivory tower that a bishopric can often be. Are they planning to visit us?"

"Yes, she hopes in about in three weeks' time. They are so busy just now. The church is full of people praying for the King's health, and he has weddings to conduct every weekend." King Edward VII had fallen ill during a visit to Paris in March. He returned to England in April and died during the first week in May.

It is evident how much the entries in the flower show had expanded when one reads a 1910 edition of *The Oxford Times*. And here, finally, there is a glimpse into the life and talents of Emma Louisa who not only gave prizes, but in the "open to all" section came second in the Working Woman's Apron and the Chemise classes.

That year Stewart was appointed president, for the one and only time, Arthur being away in South Africa. *The Banbury Guardian*, a more reliable paper, also gave an account of the same event noting that Miss Bradshaw gave prizes for fretwork, a hearthrug made from odds and ends, knitted lace, flannelette nightgown and knitted cuffs, all things that she herself was good at making.

It seems that was not all that Emma Louisa was good at. In 1892 a concert had been held in Dr Radcliffe's school rooms in aid of the Parish Reading Room. The *Banbury Advertiser* reported that the success of the evening was almost entirely due to Messrs R.H. and J. Bradshaw and Miss Bradshaw. Emma Louisa played a piano duet from *Faust* with Mrs Langham Brookes; she sang a duet with her brother John from *The Yeoman of the Guard*, and gave a solo rendition of *Needles and Pins*. She was also on the parish council for one term in 1919. At times she is noted in the local paper as having organised a jumble sale and helped to decorate the church with fruit and vegetables for the harvest festival. Little else is known about her life and what there is has been painstakingly gleaned from photographs taken at The Grange on special occasions. We see her playing croquet, feeding the dachshunds, sawing wood with her brother, and generally joining in everything. She is also pictured on picnics and boating expeditions, and on holidays, always wearing her hat and typically bent over her sewing. A self-effacing and underrated woman.

Following Emma's death, the next review of the Steeple Aston Flower Show that same year stated that it was "held in Miss Bradshaw's grounds" with Arthur presiding, suggesting that Emma Louisa was now the Lady of the Manor. She also handed out the prizes that year and later in the evening "dancing was indulged in," as the reporter put it, at the technical school.

Then the war intervened and there is no reporting of the Steeple Aston Flower and Horticultural show until 1920 when the *Banbury Guardian* wrote that the annual flower show was held at The Grange by kind permission of Mr A.E. Bradshaw. By then Arthur had restored the bowling green in the grounds and a match was held between his local team and one fielded by Mr J. Friswell of Banbury. The paper, perhaps from discretion, failed to record the winner. It did, however, mention that later there was "bowling for a pig."

However, a few months before this show was held Emma Louisa, sadly, had died. She had woken in the night with discomfort in her stomach which had increased, by breakfast time, to severe pain. Evelyn sent for the doctor, but their regular physician was away on holiday, so a young locum attended Emma Louisa.

"Nothing much," he said, as she lay tearfully on a downstairs sofa, her face creasing in spasms. "Just an upset tummy. Don't you worry, a little rest and no food today, perhaps just some weak tea and you will be up and about in no time." He patted her hand and turned to Arthur. "I think it could be nerves," he said.

Evelyn bristled. "Emma Louisa is the least nervous person in the family. If she says she is in pain, then it is very real."

The young doctor smiled in a way she thought patronizing, collected his bag and took his leave. He raised his hat and wished them "good day," as the housekeeper opened the door.

Evelyn turned to Arthur, "I don't think that was good enough," she said. "He doesn't know Lil and I think she is really ill."

"I quite agree, I'll ask Will to get the car out immediately and take her to Oxford."

Emma Louisa was wrapped in a rug against the chill March morning air and, with Arthur, was driven at some speed to Oxford where she was taken in at the Acland Nursing Home. Originally a Home for Nurses, a proper hospital wing had been opened in 1906 with an operating theatre. Arthur had medical contacts there who had examined Evelyn following her Harley Street diagnosis of situs inversus.

By now his sister was moaning and semi-conscious. There was no surgeon in attendance, but the resident doctor listened to the symptoms as Arthur described their progression and announced he would operate at once to remove her appendix, undoubtedly the cause of the trouble.

Emma Louisa was taken away, and Arthur paced outside the building, smoking, and waiting. After two hours an exhausted doctor appeared. "It was her appendix," he said. "It had burst, and she was in a bad way."

"May I see her?"

"I think better not. She is not conscious yet. Come back tomorrow.

Rest assured we will look after her."

Arthur reluctantly left the nursing home. He had a vague feeling of familiarity as the car turned out onto the road. "Take me along the Banbury Road please, Will," he said. "I think I went to school somewhere around here."

The chauffeur drove slowly through St. Giles's and Arthur peered at the buildings, but he couldn't find his school and, still distracted with worry about his sister, told Will to take him home. He had a bad feeling about the morning and wished ever after that he had insisted on seeing his Lil for what, it turned out, would have been the last time.

The telephone rang late in the day to inform the family that Emma Louisa had died without ever regaining consciousness. Following surgery, she had suffered a cerebral haemorrhage. She was forty-seven. Arthur blamed the locum, perhaps unfairly, but there was nothing to be done. She was buried quietly, near her parents in the churchyard of St. Peter and St. Paul. The Parish Council noted her passing.

"Poor Lil, she was too young," said Stewart, as they gathered afterwards at The Grange. The children were crying, and Evelyn was miserable; she had been very fond of her sister-in-law.

"Lil was part of the fabric of this house, and of all our lives," Arthur said, raising his glass in a toast, "and she will be much missed, particularly at the flower show. Perhaps we will give a prize in her name."

Her sewing basket was kept just as she had left it with unfinished bits and pieces, on top of the piano that she had sometimes played in a corner the sunroom, the place where she had loved to sit in the morning bent over her work, dogs asleep around her.

Evelyn's father Samuel died in December the following year and was buried quietly in Steeple Aston. Lilla moved to The Grange where she lived another fourteen years.

Vice Admiral Richard Bradshaw
CB. Photo Richard Preston.

Emma Bradshaw neè Walker.
Photo Richard Preston

Taylor Walker Barley Mow Brewery.
Photo Brewers Journal 1889

Arthur Edward Bradshaw,
Moses

Violet Agnes Evelyn Phillips
Bet. Photo Richard Preston

Athur and Evelyns wedding 19.6.1914

The Reverend Thomas
Rawlinson Sale Rolly c.1903

Rolly and Kate

John Bradshaw

Robert Bradshaw, Bob

Bob and Doreen Marjorie
OBeirnes wedding 1908

Emma Louisa Bradshaw, Lil.

Joseph Henry Bradshaw Harry

Stewart Bradshaw, Uncle Cuckoo

The Grange, Steeple Aston.
Photo courtesy Martin Lipson

The Grange, an eccentric castle.
Photo courtesy Martin Lipson.

The Grange

Lil and Evelyn Carbis Bay 1915

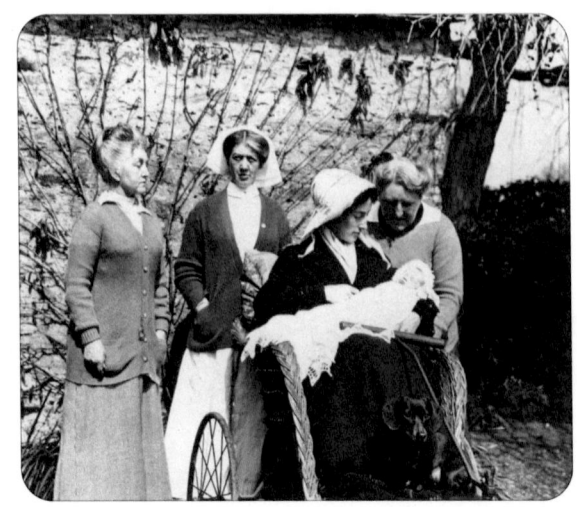

Mary Elizabeth Phillips, Nurse, Evelyn, Lil and Loveday, 3 weeks. 1915

Arthur and Evelyn

Arthur with all dachshunds

Evelyn at Henley

Rolls Royce with chauffeur Will Butler, dog and friends

Steeple Aston Flower Show Committee 1921. Steeple Aston

Steeple Aston Flower Show Arthur, Evelyn and Stewart.
Steeple Aston archive.

Evelyn - so thin she could hide behind a lamp post.

1917

On a crisp March morning the funeral of Arthur's aunt, Mary Charlotte White, took place in Oxford. Arthur hurried back to the car from the church to get out of the wind. Two dachshunds were waiting on the back seat. He was coughing and as the chauffeur made to close the door, Kate slid onto the seat beside him, pulling off her hat and poking at her hair.

"Where's Rolly?" said Arthur.

"He is rounding up the strays," Kate replied.

"He's a good man, that husband of yours."

Kate put her hat on the seat beside the dogs and smiled. "I know. I sometimes wonder what I've done to deserve him."

Arthur glanced sideways at her. "You mean apart from your organisational skills and sharp tongue?"

She smoothed the front of her coat and turned away to look out of the window, not liking to be teased. "Shall we go?"

Arthur tapped on the glass. "Home now," he said, then turning to Kate, "tell me about the Aunt Mary we have just farewelled."

"She was lovely," said Kate. "Unconventional and artistic. She was something of a botanist, went on sketching trips to Greek islands before she married and produced a couple of folios of very accomplished and beautiful drawings. She was talented and stylish, married late, in her forties I think, and had no children. Papa adored her. Her husband Robert White was a charming man too. French ancestry. A parson with a parish at Moreton Pinkney in Northampton. They suited each other very well. They came to The Grange every year as there wasn't enough money for holidays abroad, and she always did wonderful flower arrangements for the house and a couple of drawings of the garden. They are probably hanging somewhere."

"I think I know where," said Arthur. "I saw a little of her after she moved to Oxford, but not enough it seems. I wish I had known her better."

"More aunts," said Arthur. He meant Bradshaw aunts.

"Well you know Emily," Kate said. "She was a frequent visitor and such a close friend of Mama's, but she's not well now and couldn't make the journey for Mary's service. I think she will be upset by her death."

Arthur nodded.

"They were close," said Kate, "and Mary designed her London garden."

"I'm very fond of Emily," said Arthur. "Next?"

"Probably Aunt Katherine," said Kate. "She was the oldest of the girls and I'm named after her. She died just after you were born. She married John Daniell from a rich stockbroking family and lived in great luxury in London all her life. She was very social, entertained a great deal with grand dinners and knew everybody. You know the sort."

"Nothing wrong with that," said Arthur, slightly defensively. "I do a fair bit of entertaining."

"I don't mean that," said Kate. "I always found her intimidating. All Thomas and Emily's daughters were presented at court by Aunt Katherine. She'd have them to stay for the Season, take them to parties, introduce them to nice young men and lend them her pearls and ostrich feathers to meet the Queen."

Arthur smiled. "I take it you weren't presented?"

Kate looked uncomfortable. "Well, I was sent to London to stay with Aunt Katherine," she said. "Mama thought it was the right thing to do, and yes, she gave a party for me."

"Did you go to court?" Arthur persisted.

Kate rolled her eyes and fiddled at her cuffs. "Yes," she finally admitted, "I wore the feathers and met the Queen and it was all a blur, the way those things are – meant to be so important at the time and one can't remember a thing afterwards." She patted the nearest dog. "There were five children I think," she continued, changing the subject. "Henry married his first cousin Mabel Bradshaw, Thomas's daughter. And then there was Aunt Sarah. I think you were at her funeral in Sunningdale."

"I don't remember," said Arthur. "What was her story?"

"She was the quiet one," said Kate. "No obvious talents and certainly no grand entertainments. She married a clergyman called Ashton Oxenden who became the Bishop of Montreal and off they went to Canada for a spell. He was twenty years older than Sarah and well connected I believe. His father was a baronet, and he was passionate about cricket."

"Oh well, he would have got on well then with Mama's lot," said Arthur.

"I don't know that they ever met," said Kate. "Ashton had health problems. Nobody knew quite what they were, but he spent some of his youth in the south of France where he contracted a mysterious complaint which rendered him, shall we say, delicate. Anyway, under the strain of work, his health broke down in Canada, so he gave up being a bishop and returned to a small parish in England. He wrote a lot of religious books that were quite popular, and he died abroad, in Biarritz, I think. There was one daughter, Mary, an exceedingly pretty girl who married a couple of times. Her second husband was another first cousin, Humphrey Daniell."

"Was there nothing interesting about Sarah?" Arthur asked.

Kate thought for a moment. "Well yes," she said. "There was family lore that as a girl she had encountered the poet Tennyson while on holidays and fell in love with him. He wrote a verse dedicated to her, and that was it so far as he was concerned, but it was said that she never got over him and her life was somewhat blighted. We didn't dare ask her about it. She was very reticent, and deeply religious; she just didn't encourage confidences, as you can imagine. Not like Aunt Mary. You could tell or ask her anything."

"Well they all found love," said Arthur, peering out of the window and feeling for his cigarettes. "Now here we are, nearly home, dogs!"

"Is Bet alright?" asked Kate as the car turned into the gates of The Grange.

"Yes," replied Arthur. "At the moment she is. Why do you ask?"

"I just wondered why she didn't come with us this morning."

"Loveday has a fever," Arthur replied. "She was very restless, and Bet was up with her for most of the night, so she was exhausted. I suggested she stay home."

Kate looked relieved. She wondered privately if Evelyn might be having another baby but given her internal problems, it didn't seem likely.

In fact, Evelyn was not pregnant at that time, but she was later in the year, and Kathleen Eira was born the following March.

"What are your boys doing?" Arthur asked suddenly as the car came to a stop.

Kate looked up, surprised. "Tom is in the Royal Tank Corps," she said. "In France, I think. Rolly worries all the time but I feel he will be safe, and he has an ear for languages so that might be useful. Jack looks like following him into something military, but he's only fourteen so not just yet."

Arthur nodded. "Well done," he said, as half a dozen dogs crowded around the car, barking at their return. The war was on everyone's mind, but they seldom spoke of it. He could see Evelyn standing at the window in a striped dress, holding Loveday. He waved, and she lifted a hand in return, then she turned back into the room.

The chauffeur opened the door. Arthur stepped down from the car and turned to offer his hand to Kate as she gathered her hat and prepared to follow.

Emma Louisa was standing at the top of the steps, waiting for them. The tide of dogs surged past her. She seemed flustered and upset.

"What is it, Lil?" said Arthur.

"Betsy's gone, and Mabel," she said.

"Gone where?"

"To join the Women's Land Army." Emma Louisa burst into tears.

Arthur put his arm around her. "They haven't gone far," he said. "They will be working near the village, you'll see. The war effort needs them. They are young and strong, and Mabel knows horses, so she will be particularly useful when it comes to ploughing. Don't worry. They'll be back."

Emma Louisa sniffled. "When?"

"When the war is over," said Arthur, adding under his breath, *can't be soon enough.* "Come now, we can manage, let's go in to lunch." And he guided her gently through the door, followed by Kate, as Evelyn came down the stairs to join them.

In October Arthur was delighted when Dick distinguished himself by winning the championship silver cup for the best selection of vegetables at the annual RHS show in London. He also won nine first prizes in a large competition, reported in the Oxfordshire Weekly News. I wonder where he finds the time, thought Arthur, as he went looking for the gardener to offer his congratulations. Dick was in the greenhouse clearing up the last of the tomatoes to be bottled by his wife. He nodded to Arthur and the two men shook hands, lit cigarettes, and leaned against the wooden boxes.

"Very well done," said Arthur, "RHS championship, can't get any better than that."

"Same vegetables as I put on your table every day," said Dick.

"I know, how lucky are we!"

Tom Sale was indeed in the Tank Corps in France and had a very bad time of it. He had attended Eagle House prep school, followed by Marlborough College, and in 1917 he entered military service at the army training centre at Pirbright in Surrey, Officer Cadet Battalion. In November that year he passed into the Tank Corps and in early January 1918 he was sent to France. By 1919, at the age of twenty, he was a lieutenant, and the following year he retired from military service.

When he came to The Grange that summer with Rolly and Kate, both Arthur and Evelyn were appalled by his appearance. He was very thin, his hands trembled, he said he was unable to eat, nor could he sleep because of the recurring nightmares, and he jumped at the slightest noise. His anxiety was evident in every gesture. He seemed to be constantly on the verge of panic and nobody knew what to do. He refused to talk to anyone about his war experience.

Evelyn consulted Ailey. It was a huge problem apparently, called shell shock. "There were special hospitals," she said, "where, during the conflict, the object was to get the traumatised soldiers back into the front line as quickly as possible. Rest, diet, massage, and electric shock treatment were standard practice. Occupational training and the inculcation of 'masculinity' were also part of the regime."

In the early years of the war it was thought that shell shock was the result of a physical injury to the nerves, from being exposed to heavy bombardment, for example, or being buried alive. However, it was soon recognised that many soldiers suffered the symptoms of shell shock without having been in the front lines. Medical officers increasingly began to emphasise psychological factors as cause for a breakdown.

Ernest Jones, President of the British Psycho-Analytic Association, explained that war constituted an official abolition of civilised standards. Men were not only allowed but encouraged to indulge in a kind of behaviour that is "abhorrent to the civilized mind." Four-fifths of the men who entered hospital suffering from shell shock were never able to return to military duty. By the end of the war the army had dealt with 80,000 cases. The return to civilian life also produced psychological conflict and frequently brought on severe neurosis that hadn't been evident on the battlefield.

Kate was beside herself with anguish and her lips were raw from constant chewing. The laughing, happy child Tom had been was a distant memory. While Rolly prayed and she was comforted by Evelyn, Arthur sat with Tom in the garden where he had chased his brother all those years ago, dogs collected at their feet, smoking, and waited for Tom to speak. But he remained silent. Arthur, too, spoke to Ailey and she said perhaps he would talk to a professional, a psychoanalyst who practised the Talking Cure.

"It could be effective," she said, "but it takes time."

Rolly was in favour. "Anything," he said, "anything that might bring some hope of order to the chaos of his poor, tortured mind."

But Kate, though desperate, was sceptical, and rightly so as it turned out, as Tom refused to see or talk to anyone. He may have felt shame, as many did, a tremendously hard thing to express, and it seems he never got over the ordeal.

In 1924 he sailed for America, arriving in New York in April. On the passenger list he was designated "single" and it was recorded that he spoke English, French, and German. During the next twelve years he sailed back and forth between America and England several times.

In August 1927 Rolly, Kate and the girls sailed on the *Baltic* to New York to visit Tom, but there was no persuading him to return permanently. He married Gladys Corinne Denton in December 1929 and moved to California where he lived, and worked as a travel agent in Los Angeles, until his death in 1959. There were no children.

***

"We need to commemorate the flower show committee," said Arthur, at its meeting in 1921. "We shall have a photograph taken."

There were twenty men on the committee that year – the women still limited to baking, sewing and helping to hand out the prizes – and so they arranged themselves around Arthur, who sat, feet firmly planted, in the middle of the front row with a dachshund on his lap, in the garden of The Grange. He thought briefly of Emma Louisa who had died the year before, and how much she had loved the flower show, often entering her handiwork, and once winning the table decoration section.

"Look at the birdie," said the photographer, and Arthur returned to the present and concentrated on keeping the dog still.

Afterwards he shook hands with everyone, and when they had left, he sat on in the garden. He lit a cigarette and listened to the wind in the trees. I am lucky, he thought, to have all this, and now a newborn son to inherit it.

The thought of Richard, who would be called Bobby, made him smile; born a few months ago he was just a little thing, but already so full of character.

A small surge of dogs arrived at his feet. The bull terrier laid his head on Arthur's thigh, jaws working. Arthur felt in his pockets for a biscuit but finding only crumbs; he rose and led the little gang across the lawn and back to the house.

"I think it went well," he said to Evelyn later that evening. "All their shoes were polished and a few even wore buttonholes. I wore a dog."

The flower show in August went off without a hitch. Dick Wadham, as always, had the gardens at The Grange at their summer best. Various brothers and their wives came to stay. Arthur presided at lunch, and the entries in all sections were gratifyingly large. It was a part of the fabric of village life; no one could remember a time when there wasn't a flower show. The local paper, the *Banbury Guardian*, reported the event, as always, meticulously cataloguing the prize winners in each section.

In 1922 the show was held on a Wednesday, 23rd August. The day was fine. Everyone in the neighbourhood attended, a new aerial railway provided entertainment, and all seemed quite as usual. The *Banbury Guardian* reporter was dozing in a corner of the tent where Arthur was presiding at luncheon, when he suddenly heard from the president that he was shortly leaving the village. The reporter came to with a jerk and started scribbling furiously. The news was received with general regret, he wrote, because the inhabitants of Steeple Aston have good reason to be grateful for all the Bradshaws have done for the village. That wasn't the half of it. Arthur had kept this news from even some members of his family.

Where was he going? And why? In response to this bombshell, the reporter added, a committee member, Mr Porter, rose promptly to his feet to propose the health of the president, emphasising the long association the Bradshaw family had with the parish and district, and the great interest they had taken in all parochial activities.

In responding to the toast, a somewhat emotional Arthur now spoke publicly about his impending departure, a fact which he said he very deeply regretted in view of his life-long association with the village. He wished the society continued prosperity and hoped one day that he would return to his old home. Then he sat down. Evelyn lent across and patted his hand. The proceeding completed, the show was thrown open to the public, and the news was all around the village in half an hour.

The *Oxfordshire News* reporting on the same event also mentioned that Arthur's impending departure from the village was received with general regret but offered no further explanation. Evelyn won first prize for a bottle of fruit. Dick Wadham's wife, clearly a baker, won for her fruit cake, scones and a pot of jam, with second prizes in the rock cakes and ginger biscuits sections.

Did he leave?

According to the parish council records, Arthur was on the council from April 1922 for six consecutive three-year terms. In spite of his initial reluctance Arthur had become a staunch churchgoer; he joined the parish council and was involved in parochial matters. In 1923 he attended meetings in January, March, and October, so whatever plans he had for leaving Steeple Aston seem to have been abandoned. Suffice to say that in 1924 Arthur attended the April and November council meetings, and he sent, rather than took, sporting equipment to his club in South Africa. He was also present at the meeting of the Ancient Order of Foresters in 1924 where he was elected treasurer. In 1925 the local newspaper reported on the annual meeting of the Bradshaw Bowls League at which Arthur, as President, was presented with "a handsome clock in appreciation of his kindness" and a framed photograph of the preview year's winners.

Arthur was also President of the Flower Show in 1925; his lunch address, reported in the Banbury Guardian, included the information that he thought the potatoes were better even than those exhibited in the Oxford Show. However, at the flower show in 1926, in response to Bob's toast to the Society, Arthur, who was presiding at lunch said it was some years since he had been present and he very much appreciated the way the society had gone forward, largely due to Dick Wadham; the show undoubtedly wouldn't happen without him.

"It's a pleasure to work for such a good president," said Dick, seizing the opportunity to make the speech he'd wanted to for years. "The Bradshaw family is the mainstay of the Horticultural Society and has been ever since Admiral Richard's day. Thanks also are due to Mr John and Mr Stewart for their kindness." It should be noted that Arthur's friend and Patron of the flower show, George Villiers, had died aged just fifty the year before. This even had shaken Arthur up and left a gap that doesn't appear to have been filled.

It could be assumed that the flower show was conducted by the two brothers during Arthur's mysterious absence. The following year the show was held during a violent thunderstorm, and the Banbury Guardian reported that "Mr A. Bradshaw had come home specially for the event." There is no explanation for his absence from the village between 1922 and 1927, although for most years during that time he attended either the parish council or other events, dutifully reported in local newspapers, so he can't have been too far away.

In December 1927, Arthur Bradshaw applied to be admitted to the Freedom of the City of London in the Worshipful Company of Bakers and was accepted. Why he chose the Bakers is not known, but clearly it had nothing to do with bread and everything to do with networking and charity. His older brothers were members of the Company of Brewers and it may be that Arthur wished to carry out his charitable works – for that can be the only reason he joined a guild – separately from them. As brewers one can assume they would have used the Guild for business. It may also have been another reason for Arthur to go to London to stay at his club and later, to visit Wartski.

Arthur became profoundly committed to Freemasonry and it seemed to have been one of his chief delights, beginning in London early on with the Clapton Lodge. His generosity extended to Masonic charities to all degrees: Craft, Royal Arch and Mark Masonry. He filled many high offices in Freemasonry throughout the Oxford area in the Craft Chapter Mark, was a member of the Alfred Mark Lodge Oxford, and an original founding member and the first Senior Warden of the Calthorpe Lodge in Banbury in 1930, and Master the following year. He was also founder of the Mandeville Lodge, and Past Master of both the Marlborough Lodge, Woodstock, and the Royal York Lodge of Perseverance in London.

He also loved The Grange, and was deeply involved in charity at home; he sat on the parish council, the Banbury Rural District Council, the Ancient Order of Foresters, the Steeple Aston Agricultural Society, Dr Radcliffe's School, President of the Steeple Aston football club, and the Woodstock Scout Troop where he was chairman and a generous supporter from its inception in 1922, and various bowling clubs. Abroad he was a member of the Olympic Sports Club and two other golf clubs in Cape Town and a donor of trophies to each one. His generosity was somewhat counter balanced by personal extravagance.

However, even with all his interests, his family always came first, and he and Evelyn were a devoted couple.

The children, Eira, Loveday and Bobby, led an idyllic life at The Grange. With thirty acres to roam and play in, growing up with all Arthur's dogs – the dachshunds being low to the ground were perfect for small children – and plenty of people around to look after them, their early childhood was perfect.

At Christmas there was the big treat to look forward to, a trip to London to see the Pantomime. In the 1920s Cinderella was the favourite, along with Bo Peep and Queen of Hearts. In the 1930s Aladdin was top of the bill, followed closely by Snow White, Red Riding Hood, Mother Goose, and Puss in Boots. The whole family went to the Panto. They cheered the Dame and hissed at the villain, and had supper afterwards before usually heading home, but sometimes they stayed with Aunt Doreen overnight and were taken to see the lights in Regent Street. For the next few weeks, "he's behind you," was their favourite phrase, particularly when Arthur was pretending to creep up on someone, though the dogs, always in attendance, often gave him away first.

At home at The Grange for Christmas, Evelyn always visited the families on the estate and took them a Christmas Box. On Christmas Eve the children were kept out of the big hall while an enormous tree was brought in by Dick and the gardeners, and decorated by Arthur,

Evelyn, and the staff. Presents were piled beneath it and the candles lit, then the children, whose excitement built to fever pitch as they tried to peer through a crack in the door, were finally allowed in, to their great delight. Cook produced a tray of hot mince pies and Arthur poured everyone a glass of punch, and when John and Mary Kathleen or Aunt Doreen was staying, one of them would played the piano and everyone sang carols until it was time for the children to go to bed. Presents were not opened until after Church on Christmas Day.

"Where's Daddy?" Loveday climbed into her chair at the breakfast table. Ailey put a bowl of porridge in front of her and reached for the cream.

"He's sitting with one of the dogs," she said. "Been up all night."

Eira broke in. "It's Lulu," she said.

"What's wrong with Lulu?"

"Very old age," said Ailey, who didn't believe in protecting children from life's misfortunes. "She is dying, and your father will sit with her until the end."

"Will she go to heaven?" Eira was brimming with tears

"I expect so." Ailey was not hard-hearted. "She will certainly go to the dog graveyard up by the stables."

"Can we go?"

"Go where?" said Evelyn coming into the room

"Lulu is dying," said Loveday

"Yes, I know, darling, it is very sad but she is so old and tired now; she just wants to sleep."

"We want to go to the graveyard with Daddy," said Loveday

Evelyn looked stricken, "Oh, I'm not sure" she began.

"I think that's a good idea," said Ailey, "we will all go." And she nodded firmly at Evelyn.

The small procession from the house wound its way up to the stables in the late afternoon. Arthur was carrying Lulu, wrapped in an old linen sheet, followed by Loveday and Eira carrying flowers they had picked with Evelyn's help. She and Ailey brought up the rear. All the other dogs had been shut in.

"We don't need any more digging," said Arthur.

Charlie Hart had dug a hole and stood in respectful silence as the little funeral party approached.

Loveday looked around. She counted four small headstones. She realised she had seen them before but had never thought about what they meant. "That's a lot of dogs already buried," she said to her father. He smiled.

"Still got six left," he said, and laying the bundle carefully into the prepared space, he stepped back and said, "Lulu was a good dog. She loved her family; and chasing rabbits. She had a wonderful life and now she rests in peace." He turned to the girls. "Put your flowers on Lulu now," but they both held back.

"It's alright," said Ailey, "we'll put them on afterwards."

Arthur nodded, picked up a spade and he and Charlie gently replaced the earth in the grave.

When it was finished the girls placed their flowers on the little mound and Evelyn turned them towards the house. "Come along," she said, "time for tea."

"Why isn't Daddy coming?" Eira was looking back to where Arthur stood beside the grave, the sun setting behind him.

"I expect he wants to say a bit more goodbye," said Loveday.

✳✳✳

"I have ordered a Rolls Royce," said Arthur at breakfast to no one in particular. He snapped the newspaper and laid it on the table, looking around at the assembled company and noting their expressions with satisfaction. It was the day after the boat race. His two brothers had gathered for breakfast – the wives preferred a tray in bed – Kate and Rolly, and Ailey who always rose early, rearranged their faces. The children had finished and been released to play in the garden.

"But you already have two motor cars," said Bob.

"Yes," said Arthur, "but neither the Lanchester nor the Wolseley tourer are nearly big enough to convey the house parties who gather here for Ascot and Henley. With the chauffeur they both only seat three."

"We do bring our own cars," said Stewart quietly.

"I know," said Arthur, "but from now on the ladies will arrive in style. I am sending Will Butler to Derby for special training to learn how to drive it. The company insist on it." He lit a cigarette and offered the remaining crusts of toast to the dogs under the table. The bull terrier sitting closest took them all and the dachshunds yapped in protest.

"Give me your toast," Arthur said to Kate, "or there will be a fight."

Evelyn paused in the door on her way to confer with Cook. "Can you move to the sunroom dear?" she said to Arthur. "It is after ten and they want to clear up and lay for luncheon. We have another six coming".

"Good," said Arthur. "Croquet then, this afternoon." And he rose, calling to the dogs and followed by the straggling family, left the dining room, humming.

"I'm off to London this afternoon," Stewart called after him, "I need to make arrangements for my dinner. I'll be back on Thursday." A keen and successful rower himself, as the result of a substantial winning bet on an Oxford crew, he had started holding a dinner on the Tuesday after the boat race which, limited to only sixteen guests, took place annually for fifty years.

Arthur waved. "Have fun. We'll look after Clarie. Are you racing next weekend?"

"Yes, of course." Stewart never missed a meeting. "Newmarket, and we are taking friends."

Kate gathered up the papers and caught up with Arthur, slipping her arm through his. "I saw you talking to Roger Daniell at the boat race," she said. "He has a Rolls Royce. Does he think well of it?"

"Best car in the world," said Arthur, "and the Daniells would know. Clever stockbrokers – made a fortune and kept it through three generations so far. Can't say that about many in our family."

Kate looked at him. "Your brothers have done very well at the brewery," she said. "They have hardly squandered Mama's inheritance."

"True," said Arthur and he thought fleetingly of Harry who had been bound for the navy but changed course and had taken off for adventures in Africa.

"How are we related?" Kate broke into his thoughts

"The Daniells are cousins," said Arthur, "and each generation has married a Bradshaw. Not Roger though. He married Kathleen Monsell, a Catholic, whose father was Chief Constable of the Metropolitan Police."

"Rolly knows the son," said Kate. "Bolton Eyres-Monsell, he was at Stubbington House with Stewart and Harry, and is now an MP and, I think, something in the Admiralty."

"Can't say I care much for politics," said Arthur, opening the door to the sunroom as the dogs surged past. "Let's go in here and finish the papers in peace."

He settled with *The Times*, the dachshunds piled on top of each other in a patch of sunlight while the three bull terriers Prempeh – named for an African King of the Ashanti who fought against Britain – Sheila and Pixie, sat protectively at Arthur's feet. Beside his chair was a small photo album devoted entirely to these three dogs. They were much loved by Arthur but not by the rest of the family. The dachshunds, however, were universally liked.

Kate sat and watched Evelyn in the distance, moving slowly along the border with a basket, picking camellias, daffodils, and daphne. When the basket was filled, she made her way to the steps leading to the sunroom.

Arthur rose to open the door and smiled at her. "Lovely flowers, my dear," he said.

At that moment Stewart came into view and bounded up the steps after Evelyn. "Who is coming to lunch?" he asked.

Arthur looked vague. "Just some locals. Why? Do you have someone you'd like to invite?"

"You remember young Stuart Bradshaw? You must have met him in South Africa. Hugh and Linty's son."

"Yes of course," said Arthur. "Very nice boy, quiet, went to Rugby, I think. I asked him here a couple of times, but he always went to his aunt Evelyn in London".

"Well now he's up at Oxford," said Stewart, "and it's but a step away."

"Good, we'll have him over for Ascot, shall we?" Arthur looked at Evelyn, who nodded. "He must be about twenty-three, might keep Eira amused."

"Oh please," said Evelyn, "don't start weaving a romance for the girl."

"He's very good looking," said Stewart, teasing her. Then he became serious: "Perhaps not Ascot, he's not a racing man and I don't know he'd have the right clothes. Henley might be better. Less formal."

"Quite right," said Arthur, "Henley it is, but how do you know so much about him?"

"I play golf with him and a couple of his friends occasionally, but forget the romance, I believe he's madly in love with Lord Northbourne's daughter, Mary."

"But she's married," objected Evelyn, who read the society columns in the papers, "to one of the Llewellyn-Davies, you know, the Peter Pan children."

"Perhaps he just adores her from afar," said Arthur. "Let's get him over. Is his golf any good?"

Stewart grinned. "He has a blue."

"Oh good lord," said Arthur, "I'm not going to play him!"

Evelyn collected her basket and left the room. She knew she wasn't very good at flower arrangements, but the daffodils could stand alone in a vase and luckily camellias arranged themselves in her experience, so the lunch table would be decorated with alternate vases of blue and pink without much assistance from her. Best to put the daphne in the hall, she thought. Lovely though it is, their strong perfume was not conducive to the enjoyment of food. Emma had taught her that.

Stuart Bradshaw borrowed a car and came to stay for Henley. He was a definite asset to the house party; tall, good looking with a quiet charm, he joined in everything and it was obvious that he was good, not just at golf, but all sports. He was reading law, and during the next couple of years was frequently invited to The Grange for weekends. After graduation he got a job in the City and moved to London, so they saw less off him.

"A pity," said Arthur to Evelyn, "I really like the man."

Then suddenly, Stuart was gone. "Left his job?" said Arthur incredulous, "Whatever possessed him?"

"A woman," said Evelyn, who had been gossiping with London friends. "He has run off with another married woman, a Margaret Carbutt, who has left her husband, and two small daughters in the nursery. And her jewels on the dressing table," she added, having a passion for such details.

Arthur was stunned. "Where did they go?" he said.

"Stuart has gone to Australia. His mother has family out there, farming I think, and Mrs Carbutt has gone to friends in Prussia I believe, to wait for her divorce. Then I expect she will follow him."

Arthur shook his head at such folly. He thought of Hugh and Linty Bradshaw; he had spent many happy weekends with them in South

Africa and he remembered that Linty had parents in Australia. Stuart was their only child and if he did marry and settle in Australia they would most probably emigrate to be near him. Hugh must be near to retiring, he thought. What would they think of this scandal? It seemed out of character with the Stuart he knew, had in fact known since he was a small boy. He had always seemed a model of propriety. Talented too. A damned waste, thought Arthur.

He sighed, lit a cigarette, then humming Land of Hope and Glory which always alerted the dogs to a walk, set off to inspect the bowling green, collecting his hat on the way out. It was a blustery day and he turned up his collar. The dogs ran after him, ears flapping.

Evelyn watched him go. Hands plunged deep in her pockets, she rocked back on her heels and thought about the scandal. It is always the quiet ones that surprise you, she thought. She had liked Stuart. He had very good manners and seemed sincere. In spite of his obvious sporting prowess, he was modest, and she approved of that. He had teased her daughters gently but had been light-hearted and even-handed in his dealings with his cousins, enough to discourage any romantic notions they might have harboured. Just as well, she thought, as his interests had lain exclusively with married women.

Arthur crossed the lawn and stopped to speak to Dick who was directing new plantings in the vegetable garden. There were six under-gardeners and Arthur had wondered briefly if they were all necessary.

He mentioned this to Dick once, who thought for a bit and then said, "Well, three of them are young, and in training like, and you have nearly thirty acres here. It's a show piece this garden is. The woodland and the bowling green take a bit of maintaining. Then there's the vegetables and flower borders, and all the village comes here to the fetes and garden shows and to play bowls, so I reckon its worth every one of us."

"That's what I wanted to hear," said Arthur, and the subject was never mentioned again. The brewery paid the wages without question and the brothers were always complimentary on the way the estate looked on their frequent visits. Dick had a cottage on the North Side adjacent to the service entrance gates. The butler Charlie Hart lived in the Stables cottage and the chauffeur Will Butler also had a cottage on the North Side. Opposite his cottage was a pair of stately wrought iron gates, painted dark green, and one of his jobs was to open them in the morning and close them every night. When the Second World War came, the gates were requisitioned and taken away to be melted down. They were never replaced.

"There was another family scandal, I remember, some years ago," said Arthur that evening, stirring his coffee. "Also, on Aunt Emily's side of the family so not as close to home, which scandalised Mama and entertained us at the time."

Evelyn looked up expectantly, and Arthur poured her a small glass of madeira. "Do tell me."

"Hugh Halkett, Emily's nephew and a good-looking chap, married an American heiress, Sarah Phelps Stokes, whose father was a millionaire stockbroker. She became a baroness on her marriage and with her settlement he then had enough money to leave his job with Rothschilds and stand for Parliament in Chester. When he failed to gain a seat, they returned to London and the marriage fell apart. Her health was not always good and he was often out and about with other women, dining at Rules."

"What is Rules?" interrupted Evelyn.

Arthur was about to say something sharpish, then realised that she knew very little of London, let alone its dining establishments. "The oldest restaurant in London, an institution, frequented by society. No possibility one could dine there and not be seen. Hugh was frequently spotted with his latest conquest. Very humiliating. Anyway, luckily there were no children – part of the problem I suppose – and Sarah sued for divorce, citing infidelity and brutality, claiming at times he kicked her like a dog. The divorce was granted immediately. Then she then went further and sued for the return of the Stokes millions settled on her at the time of the marriage. She was successful, I believe, and retired to live in the Adirondacks in America."

"What happened to him?" Evelyn was on the edge of her chair.

"Hugh went out to South Africa almost straight away, in disgrace and penniless. He met up with Stuart's parents, and then rather rashly joined the army. He was killed shortly afterwards."

Evelyn sat back and twisted her hands. "That is a sad story, but Hugh probably deserved what he got."

Arthur was surprised. She was usually more forgiving. "They do say that Hugh had a bad riding accident the year before his marriage," said Arthur. "He fell off a horse in Hyde Park and fractured his skull. Those who knew him well, like Emily's daughter Evie, said his personality changed after that. You never know. Still it doesn't excuse his flaunting his mistresses, and kicking his wife was unforgivable."

Evelyn sighed. Obviously the Halketts had not been a compatible couple. She knew that Arthur, despite the odd burst of bad temper, would never, ever hit her, or his children, or even the dogs however naughty. Or would he?

Arthur was in a temper. It was not yet a rage, but he was building towards an explosion. It was a dog that started the train of events. It usually was, but which dog was the ringleader? He couldn't chastise them all, and besides the entire pack had slunk away in a thoroughly guilty manner when Arthur came into the kitchen and discovered, not only the remains of a sheepskin slipper, but also a partially shredded favourite cushion embroidered by his beloved sister Lil. He felt a wave of anger. The slipper he could endure but the cushion was a real loss. Why? When they had each other to play with, and bones and the garden, what had possessed them to attack his possessions? It had been raining for some days admittedly and the dogs had been confined, but still.

"Naughty," he shouted, as Evelyn appeared in the door, the dogs scattered and the children, who heard the shouting, retreated upstairs.

She took in the scene, then as he bent to gather up the remains of the cushion a cupboard door swung open silently above him and, before she could warn him, he stood up and banged his head, hard, against it. He yelled in pain, and the dogs retreated further into the house. Evelyn crossed the room to where he was standing, seething, holding the remnants of the cushion.

"Let me look at your head, Mo," she said quietly. "It's bleeding a bit. Come with me and I'll dress it for you." Arthur, who was fighting to control himself, was about to brush her off, but thought better of it.

"No biscuits for that lot today," was all he managed to say grimly.

Evelyn took the cushion from him and examined the damage. "I think Mary who does the kneelers for the church might be able to restore this," she said, trying to be helpful. Arthur sighed, his anger abating, but the day was not over.

Head cleaned and bandaged, but beginning to ache, Arthur went into his office. Opening the mail, he found a letter from the secretary of one of the associations of which he was president, advising him that the accountant had been helping himself to funds. It was not a large amount, but it was carelessness that nobody had picked it up before. The rage over the dogs was still simmering, and this letter caused another surge. He reached for the telephone and spent a short ten minutes advising the accountant that his services were terminated, that he would get no reference from Arthur and furthermore, all monies were to be returned forthwith or it would be a police matter. Then he slammed down the phone, knowing it was childish, but giving vent to his frustration relieved his tension somewhat.

Feeling slightly better, he noticed that the rain had stopped so he fetched his walking stick. A few of the dogs were now sitting expectantly at the kitchen door, but he ignored them as he shrugged into his coat and, leaving the disgraced dogs shut in, set off for the woodlands. His head was still throbbing slightly as he crossed the lawn; the grass was very wet underfoot and squelched with every step. It felt odd not to be accompanied by his tribe. I should inspect the "poly walk", he thought.

Created by his mother this path, planted with primroses and polyanthus, wound through the woodland. It was a place of enchantment where the girls had looked for fairies when they were little. He recalled the only time he remembered Harry being in trouble was when he rode his horse along the path. Startled by a rabbit, the pony had backed up and trampled on the flowers and Harry was banned from riding for a week. Arthur smiled at the memory. He slackened his pace looking for little clumps of newly washed flowers where a weak sunlight shafted through the trees, picking out glimmerings of yellow.

Then a bird flashed overhead and, as he glanced up, he failed to notice a fallen log and tripped, putting out his hand to break the fall he felt something snap. That was the final straw. Arthur shouted an obscenity, then rolled onto his back in a patch of wet primroses, emotions stripped bare, holding his arm and feeling tears of self-pity welling. He dimly heard a skylark high above working itself into a frenzy, but though he would normally have listened with wonder he just lay for some time, cursing to the heavens.

Finally, exhausted, damp, and in some pain, he struggled to his feet and set off for the house cradling his arm against his chest. Halfway across the field he was met by a pack of dachshunds. Dick had gone to the kitchen door with a bucket of freshly dug potatoes and Cook opened at his knock, letting the waiting dogs loose. They scampered around Arthur with delight. He leant against a big tree in the middle of the field. A light rain was again falling.

"Surely nothing more could happen today," he said to the dogs, who wagged in unison and followed him back to the house.

The local doctor confirmed a broken collar bone and tugged it into place, immediately easing his discomfort. Later that evening, his arm in a sling, he sat with a whisky, the dogs around him. "Sorry dogs," he said, "not your fault."

"What do you mean?" said Evelyn.

He recounted the day's misadventures; the destroyed cushion leading to a crack on the head, the dishonest accountant and then his fall in the woodlands.

"Three in a row," said his superstitious wife, "that's an end to it then."

In South Africa in February 1922, following a drop in the world price of gold, companies decreased wages and attempted to weaken the colour bar to enable the promotion of cheaper black labour to skilled positions. A disastrous strike led to an armed uprising by white miners known as the Rand Rebellion. Jan Smuts crushed the rebellion with 20,000 troops, artillery, tanks, and bombers. This action cost many lives and caused a political backlash which led, in 1924, to the overthrow of the Smuts ministry.

On the sporting front however, the good news was that Arthur had succeeded in obtaining a supply of squash rackets and balls and the game had taken on a new lease of life. The Olympics knew what was important.

In August 1924 Arthur received a letter from Vollie van der Bijl, the President of the Olympic Sports Club, which read in part that, with the unanimous approval of the Committee, Arthur was to be made an honorary life member of the club.

He consulted Garrard's in Albemarle Street, renowned for their sporting trophies and for handling the Cullinan diamond. "One of my sporting clubs in South Africa has done me an honour and, as it is also the 21st birthday of the club, I think I will give them a trophy," he said. "I need a nice bit of silver."

"Leave it to me," said the director, "I will find something."

The next time Arthur called at the shop there were four silver cups lined up for him to choose from. He looked them over carefully and selected a George II double-handled, sterling silver cup and had it mounted on a plinth with spaces for shields where the winners' names could be engraved. He offered the cup to be played for annually at any game decided on by the committee. The offer was accepted by the club and for its initiation it was decided the Bradshaw Cup would be a golf competition. This was held at Hout Bay in August 1925 on a wet and blustery day. Arthur was not present. The president won the competition – a popular win it must be said. The Bradshaw Cup remains a golf trophy to this day.

It would be nice to think this was the highlight of the club's 21st birthday, but alas, Arthur's present was completely overshadowed in the club annals by a visit in July from HRH The Prince of Wales, when he played a game of squash with Captain Clifford. Furthermore, before the game, when it was discovered that rain had covered part of the court where they were to play, the Royal Person took off his shoes, rolled up his trousers and helped in the mopping up. He then signed the Visitors' Book and presented the Barlow, the Club Steward, with a gold piece which he fastened to his watch chain and kept in his pocket for the rest of his life, to show to everyone who asked to see it.

As the girls were growing, being close in age they often made friends with the same people. Two of these were Mitford girls: Unity, known as Bobo, and Jessica, known as Decca. Another family where everyone had a nickname.

Arthur was friends with the eccentric, anti-social, right-wing David Mitford; both men were tall, upstanding, blue-eyed, handsome, and devoted to their dogs. David Mitford, renowned for his appalling temper, was once persuaded to take the older children to Stratford to see Romeo and Juliet; he cried at the end and then flew into a rage because the play had ended badly. All the fault of that padre, a damned papist, he kept saying in the car going home.

Arthur and Evelyn were invited to dine at Asthall Manor in the early days of their marriage. Also staying in the house was David's mother, Lady Redesdale. During a pause in the conversation she turned to Arthur and inquired how long had the Bradshaws been out of trade. Sydney Mitford quickly created a diversion and Arthur was saved from having to answer the question.

He forgot the incident, however Evelyn felt he had somehow been insulted. Already intimidated by the Mitfords she attempted to retreat from further contact and, when it was forced upon her, was unable to use their Christian names, calling them always Lord and Lady Redesdale. She confided her unease to Ailey early in her acquaintance with the family who said, "Oh, just wear more perfume, Bet, it will give you confidence." Then seeing Evelyn's dismay, became serious and added, "Let Arthur go and visit them on his own, you don't need to be spending time with people who make you hold your breath."

The girls, however, were sometimes invited to spend the day, first at Asthall Manor, and later when the family moved to Swinbrook, where David Mitford built an enormous three-storied house. Will Butler would drive them the twenty-five miles in the morning and collect them before dinner. Loveday was enthralled by the house, the six girls and Tom, the menagerie of dogs, donkeys, horses, chickens, guinea pigs, goats, an orphaned lamb and a tame ring dove which flew above Decca's head as she cycled to the village. Sydney Mitford intrigued her, especially at lunch when she exercised by circling her arms and yawning in the belief that it aided her digestion. However, they both kept clear of Farve, as he was called by his children, particularly when there was shouting. "Daddy shouts too," said Eira, "mostly at the dogs."

"It's probably the Germans," said Decca, but offered no further explanation.

One day Loveday came home with something new. Evelyn, who knew the girls had taken no money with them, asked her where it had come from. Had one of the girls, Bobo perhaps, given her the nice bangle? Loveday shook her head. Well, her mother persisted, where did it come from?

Loveday grew a little pink. Then, "I took it," she said in a small voice.

Evelyn was appalled. "Took it? Took it from where? One of the girls?" Loveday shook her head again. "I'm fetching your father," she said, "we must get to the bottom of this."

There were tears, but little by little the story emerged that the Mitford girls' governess, Miss Dell, had been instructing her charges in the art of shop lifting. They in their turn had shown Loveday, but Eira had stayed firmly outside the village shop. Arthur was uncertain what to do beyond suggesting that the girls didn't visit in the daytime, but as it turned out, Sydney Mitford had found out and Miss Dell was dismissed.

As they grew up the girls were often invited. "They are the same ages more or less," said Evelyn, "shouldn't I go too?"

Ailey disagreed. "No, if they think it's fun, then let them go on their own," she said, and then changed the subject. Ailey was not one to dwell.

1929-31

In the three years of their travels Arthur and Evelyn visited North Africa, Italy, Switzerland, and France. While not quite a Grand Tour they were picturesque places with contrasting climates, and they toured the "sights" rather than museums, walked in the mountains and occasionally photographed each other.

In the spring of 1929 Arthur took Evelyn on what was probably her first long trip outside of England. This may have been to make up for his extended voyage on the *SS Mooltan* the previous year with Stewart and Clarie to Australia and back, Evelyn only joining them in Marseilles for the final leg. They had sailed from Southampton on the *Ruahine* bound for New Zealand on 26th April 1928.

Two weeks later brother Bob died at home. Exhaustion, cardiac failure, and lung cancer were listed as the causes of death. He was buried in the Epsom cemetery and he left Doreen well-off; £168,000 divided between her and his nephew Jack Sale. He was fifty-four. Did he know? Did the brothers know, and would they have gone to Australia if they had known?

The Christmas following his death, Doreen came to The Grange bearing a scrap book. "I didn't know he kept one," she said to Evelyn, "but do have a look at it."

"How interesting," said Arthur when Evelyn showed him. "There is nothing about our family, not a mention unless you count a photo of their wedding."

The book was full of cartoons cut from newspapers, detailed descriptions of cricket matches, and anything to do with the Walker brothers. Tucked away in the centre pages was a newspaper article about Doreen's success in winning her singles match at the Riviera tennis championships in Menton in 1924, a year when Suzanne Lenglen won the title overall in her lead up to Wimbledon.

"I didn't know you played tennis," said Arthur at breakfast the following morning.

She smiled. "I did play quite a lot at one time," she said, "but as you don't have a court here you wouldn't have seen me play."

"You could have told us," said Evelyn, "and I'm surprised that Bob didn't. We would have liked to share your triumph."

"I expect he'd have thought it was bad form," said Stewart who was listening with interest. "He was rather a dark horse, my brother, he would have kept his golf handicap a secret if he could."

"What shall we do about the girls?" said Arthur, when preparing for their cruise. "I suppose we could leave them at home but that might be rather dull. Bobby's away at school, so there would be even less entertainment at home. Perhaps they could go to Stewart and Clarie for a couple of weeks. They love Uncle Cuckoo."

"I know," said Evelyn, "they can visit Branch at Grasmere." Evelyn's brother was rector of St Oswald's fifteenth century church, a grade 1 listed building where Wordsworth was buried. His nature was somewhat brittle; he walked with a limp, and was quite opposite in character to his much-loved, cleric brother-in-law, Rolly.

When Loveday heard of this plan her reaction was immediate. "No!" she shouted, "I don't want to go to Uncle Branch, I don't like him."

Eira was also close to tears. "He hits us with his walking stick, and it really hurts."

"Who hits the children?" demanded Arthur coming into the room.

"Uncle Branch," chorused the girls.

"He doesn't mean any harm, I'm sure," said Evelyn, "I'll write to him at once."

"Please don't make us go, Daddy." Loveday was working herself up. "Uncle Branch goes thwack on our backs with his stick when he sees us. And he's as mad as a hatter, and he won't let me practice," she added, under her breath. Loveday had taken up the oboe and was having lessons. Her teacher praised her efforts and told Evelyn that her daughter had quite a talent. But she must practice, he advised, and Loveday did, every day, determined to make a career as a musician.

"That's unacceptable," said Arthur. "I shall ring him up and have a word." To the girls he said, "Under the circumstances you don't have to go. You can stay at home for now, and perhaps spend a week with Uncle Cuckoo."

"A pity," he said to Evelyn later, "the Lake District is so beautiful, and Grasmere in particular, but I cannot send the girls there if they are afraid of your brother." She opened her mouth to say something but thought better of it. With age, Evelyn had grown in self-confidence and, Arthur noticed, she could be outspoken, even eccentric; during the early days of the war when Britain went onto double summertime she refused to alter the clocks at The Grange, causing great confusion in the village. However, where her brother was concerned, aware of his shortcomings, she restrained herself.

So Arthur and Evelyn left their children at home, boarded the *Arcadian* at Southampton, and took an Atlantic Islands cruise to North Africa, stopping first at Tangier, the Pearl of the North and a destination for the artists Matisse and Delacroix, and writers Oscar Wilde – who firmly believed that "travel broadens the mind" and Andre Gide, who claimed that "it is only in adventure that some people succeed in knowing themselves."

It can be assumed that they were travelling without a camera as all the views of this cruise are commercial postcards, with one exception – a photograph of Arthur and Evelyn with their local guide in Rabat, taken by a street photographer. Evelyn is smartly dressed. Arthur, in an ice cream suit, straight out of a Graham Greene novel with white shoes and a buttonhole, leans nonchalantly on a pillar, smiling, hand in pocket. Both are wearing hats and tower over their guide who stands between them. The postcards chosen show the entrance to the Kasbah, marketplaces, white-robed figures, donkeys and laden camels, beautiful dark-eyed children, and romantic, heavily shadowed doorways. There is one view of Casablanca and the postcards also show, confusingly, the *SS Arcadian*, clearly not the one torpedoed in 1917, but formerly the good ship *Asturias*, also torpedoed in 1917, then salvaged, refurbished, refitted as a cruise ship, and renamed *Arcadian*, until finally scrapped in 1933. From Tangier they sailed on to the Canary Islands, Las Palmas and Tenerife, where the weather was milder, and collected postcards of the landscape and banana plantations.

While they were away, Kate's daughter Mary got married to Reginald Vernon Hume, an English soldier who was awarded the USA Legion of Merit during World War II. Kate was a bit put out. "You might have made the effort to come back in time," she said to Arthur, in her usual forthright manner.

"I'm really sorry," said Arthur, "but I have no control over shipping schedules."

"Katy isn't pleased," he said to Evelyn. "We must send Mary something nice. We'll go to London next week and have a look in Aspreys. They have a decent range."

Arthur was very fond of his niece. He was fond of all Kate's children, and regretted that he had so little contact with his other niece, Harry's daughter Agnes, as she and her mother remained sequestered in Devon. Arthur knew that Harry had not found his fortune in Africa and had left his wife Agnes a little over £15,000, though whether that was spoils from his prospecting or shares in the family brewery, nobody knew. He thought John might have assumed responsibility for Harry's widow.

It was a blistering summer in 1930, and the entries were down in the annual Flower show in August. As secretary, Dick Wadham reported that nearly all the local societies had, in his words, gone broke, however Steeple Aston had kept its head above water. No doubt Arthur helped. Following the show, in September he suggested to Evelyn that they take a car and one of the dogs and travel around on the Continent.

"What a lovely idea", said Evelyn, who found the sea slightly terrifying.

"Where would you like to go?"

"Switzerland," she said. Odd, thought Arthur. He thought Switzerland was mostly mountains, and that she might prefer Paris, but it would be cooler so why not?

Leaving Eira at the Wychwood School in Oxford and Loveday at home with her music, they took the Wolseley tourer, Will Butler, and a dachshund called Chamberlain, and headed for the coast. At Dover, their car was winched aboard a Townsend Ferry and deposited in Calais two hours and thirty minutes later. From there they drove to Geneva and took rooms in a hotel beside the lake.

What we know about this holiday is due mostly to Evelyn. She created the photo album and notes her presence in the photos, where she appears, as "myself". Though not entirely in sequence and some of the spelling is hit and miss, this is the most valuable record there is. Many of the pictures are beautifully composed – Switzerland is nothing if not photogenic – and even in black and white, the autumn mists rising from the lake create an ethereal atmosphere. They visited the cities of Lausanne, where the Cathedral captured Evelyn's attention, and as far north as Bern, but it is the smaller alpine villages where most pictures were taken. Leaving the car, these were visited by train. From the picturesque Villars, a ski resort, to the Gemmi Pass the dramatic mountain peaks fill most of the frames.

At Vevey they visited the Aile Castle, and at the thermal spa of Loeche les Bains, near Leukerbad, Arthur sat on the edge of a hot spring, trousers rolled to the knee, feet in the water, smoking and conversing with a Captain John Harvey doing the same. Evelyn lunched on a terrace with a Mrs and Miss Olive, guests at the Beau Rivage hotel.

"What's this supposed to do for us?" Arthur asked Captain Harvey.

"Good for something," replied the Captain, a stern-looking fellow smoking a pipe. "My feet needed a rest, all that walking up and down hills don't you know." They wiggled their legs in the warm water and smoked in silence. Arthur wondered how long before he could decently escape this very dull man.

"Any golf around here?" he asked.

"Don't know, I don't play myself. Bit of boating when the weather is good, and the wife lets me."

Arthur saw his opening, "Aha," he said, looking towards the hotel, "my wife is waving to me from the terrace, I'm afraid I must leave you, sir, it seems lunch is ready."

At Montreux where Blanche Deval had a chalet, their friend Muriel, frequently seen at The Grange, suddenly appeared in a photo on the balcony of their bedroom. Hard to imagine she had been travelling with them all along. An unidentified set of four little pictures are captioned "near the Silver Fox Farm", presumably far south of the lake as one mountain shot is labelled Mont Blanc. They stayed at Les Avants, where the first European Ice Hockey championships were held in 1910. They went hiking with Blanche, who had joined them on their holiday, and she took pictures of Arthur and Evelyn resting on the grass, alpenstocks laid aside, after a ramble in the alpine pastures. At St Legier they put up the grand Hotel Beau Rivage and finally at Villars, they stopped at the Hotel Maison Blanche. This seems to have been the end of their Swiss adventure. The weather was excellent, and the brisk mountain air may have invigorated Evelyn for there is no sign of fatigue and she seems to be present, and enjoying, every moment of the trip.

June 1931 Arthur and Evelyn again embarked on a cruise, this time to Italy, on the Japanese ship the *Suwa Maru* out of Marseille bound for Yokohama. They left the ship at Naples and stayed at the Hotel Bertolini with very fine views of the city.

The Bertolini, perched high on a cliff, featured a palm court and in its day was very grand indeed. Over time, it has ceased to be a hotel and is now a restaurant and wedding venue called Bertolini's Hall. Surprisingly, in contrast to the Swiss pictures, the early photos taken from the balcony of their hotel room show a lack of experience with the medium. We see nothing more of Naples, but there is an excursion to Pompeii with a picture of the flag-stoned way, and several photos of Vesuvius erupting satisfactorily. Although the ash-buried figures had been discovered long before, there is no evidence that Arthur and Evelyn saw them. There is one photo of Rome, suggesting a day excursion to the Eternal City: an anonymous street with a couple of grand buildings and a bus. Did they, perhaps, visit and decided that the city was too vast and overwhelming and hastily return to Napoli, as Evelyn, getting into the spirit of Italy, took to captioning it?

Their next and final destination was the Grand Hotel Quisisana on Capri. Founded as a clinic in the mid-nineteenth century by Dr George Sydney Clark and named Quisiana (here one heals), the doctor soon realised it had far more appeal to tourists than invalids and turned it into a hotel. In the early 1900s Capri, which had been popular since the days of Odysseus and Tiberius, became a mecca for high society, and royalty, politicians, actors, writers, industrialists all stayed at this hotel. Jacqueline Kennedy Onassis sailed her yacht to the marina specially to buy her white "capri" pants. Arthur and

Evelyn didn't take pictures of each other, but there are several from the window of the hotel looking up to Anacapri, as well as the piccolo marina, the famous rocks, and a few of a seaplane which had crashed dramatically into the bay and was obviously a novelty.

"We must go up there," said Arthur, looking at Anacapri.

"It looks very steep," said Evelyn.

"Yes, but there will be a cart and donkey or even a bus." In fact, there was a taxi, a Fiat, brand new with the top cut off. Arthur thought that was terrific fun and up they went. The road was precipitous and Evelyn, with her hat firmly pulled down over her ears, was too scared to look at the view.

They visited the villa of San Michele, home of the Swedish psychiatrist and celebrated writer Axel Munthe whose book, *The Story of San Michele*, had been published two years earlier. Arthur had read the book and thought it romantic but there were rumours that some of Roman artefacts in the villa had been pilfered from Pompeii during excavations. "I don't know what to think about that," he said to Evelyn. She hadn't read the book.

"Well, we can't see inside the villa anyway," she said, "but the views are breathtaking." They took pictures of the outside of the villa looking back over the landscape of Capri and made the perilous descent in the same taxi who had waited for them.

Back at the hotel Arthur ordered champagne and they sat on the terrace overlooking the Bay of Naples to watch the setting sun turn the sea gold, then pink. A small grey shadow slipped from under a nearby table and wound itself around Arthur's legs. He leaned over to stroke the cat.

"This is so lovely," said Evelyn, "do you think we will ever return?"

Arthur lit a cigarette and puffed for a minute before answering. "We can if you want to," he said, "but just think how many other countries there are we have yet to visit."

Arthur and Evelyn returned just in time for their other niece's wedding. Elizabeth Bradshaw Sale married a businessman at St Saviour's Chelsea, the same church where her sister had been married two years earlier.

There was no record of any further travel abroad for about seven years, so Evelyn put the photos into the album she started after their North African cruise, and there was much travel talk around the table. Arthur was sometimes asked why they hadn't spent more time in Rome. He replied that they had wanted a holiday by the sea and Capri had been recommended by friends. Evelyn searched Blackwell's in Oxford and found a cookery book with a few Italian recipes. Cook was persuaded to try making lasagne which was such a success it rapidly became a firm favourite with the children and often appeared at lunch as an entrée.

Rolly and Kate were now living in a vicarage in Rochdale where he was Archdeacon of St Chad's, a church whose first record dates from 1194. They were staying for the weekend and during dinner Evelyn was talking about the fun they had in Switzerland.

"I'd love a holiday abroad," said Kate.

"Why not?" said Arthur. "You must be able to take time off now, Rolly. You could go on a cruise just the two of you."

Rolly smiled. "Where would you like to go, wife of mine?"

"Italy," she replied without a moment's hesitation.

So Rolly and Kate took a holiday, without the girls, sailing to Genoa on the Royal Dutch Line *Rembrandt*. It was a success; the port enchanted them, they looked at palaces and the San Lorenzo Cathedral, even older than St Chad's, and Rolly promised they would have more holidays.

In 1927, as previously mentioned, he took the two girls and Kate to America, probably to see Tom and try, once more, to persuade him to return to England, to no avail. They returned from Canada on the

Letitia to Glasgow the same year. In 1934, he took Kate on an even longer voyage, as far as Japan. Oblivious to the politics of that country and its mounting aggression against China, they viewed Mount Fuji, enjoyed the strange food and were entranced by the delicate woodcuts and screen paintings. Kate purchased six pottery bowls which they used every day at home, and they returned to England on the P&O *Carthage*.

When Rolly retired, they left the peat bogs, the cotton mills and the coal mines of Lancashire and retired to warmer climes in the south, to Folkestone, now a rebuilt holiday resort with pleasure gardens and tourists. Rolly died the same year as John and a few days before Arthur in October 1939. Apart from John, Arthur was about the only other member of the Bradshaw family who was neither married nor buried by Rolly Sale.

At The Grange Lilla, who had lived there on and off since Samuel died, was ailing. Evelyn was worried and wanted something done, but Ailey took a pragmatic view.

"Your mother is old," she said to Evelyn, "and just fading away. She isn't in pain, but she is losing her strength. We should just make her comfortable and let nature take its course." Eira sat and read James Hilton's *Lost Horizon* to Lilla in the afternoons, which she seemed to enjoy, and she died quietly in June at the age of eighty-three and was buried with Samuel in the Steeple Aston church yard.

1935

Life at the Grange continued with a regular round of summer entertainments; Ascot, Henley, the flower show, house parties, following the seasons, until the morning that Arthur, attracted by a diamond bracelet in a window, stepped unawares into Wartski's shop and everything changed.

Following his first two purchases Arthur returned to Wartski the following week, chauffeur-driven, and bought a Fabergé figure of a man smoking, with other items, for £750. By the time Wartski organised the Exhibition of Russian Art at No. 1 Belgrave Square in June and July, Arthur was in the fatal grip of Fabergé and had purchased eighteen items which Emanuel Snowman persuaded him to lend for that exhibition. "You don't have to say where you live in the catalogue," he said. "The items can be listed care of us at Wartski."

Arthur did not attend the opening as the list of royalty and others of grandeur and renown was quite overwhelming. He chose instead to go to the exhibition the following week, hoping for a quiet look. The house in Belgrave Square was stacked, room after room with treasures such as Arthur had never seen before.

In room 4, where his snuff boxes were displayed, he experienced a shiver of delight at being in such august company, and he gazed at his objects in the display cases with such intensity that he failed to notice a flurry in the doorway, and was startled when a person arrived quietly at his elbow and, looking into the same case, said "Very pretty, are they yours?"

"Yes," said Arthur, without looking round. The speaker coughed quietly, and he turned to be confronted, to his absolute amazement, with a familiar face surmounted by a lilac toque and adorned with many ropes of pearls. A lady-in-waiting hovered. Queen Mary. He flushed, took a step backwards knocking into a display case and bowed low, trying not to show how disconcerted he was. "Your Majesty."

The Queen, who was used to people behaving oddly in her presence, just said, "I have some like that at home." Arthur wondered fleetingly which Palace she referred to as "home".

"I do admire the work of Mr. Fabergé, don't you?" Queen Mary went on, and, not waiting for an answer, "Will you walk around some rooms with me?"

Arthur later tried hard to recall every word spoken during that enchanted half hour; the Queen's interest in the displays, even pointing out a few things she had loaned.

"She couldn't have been more gracious and kinder to an unknown," he told Emanuel Snowman. "She knew I was a new collector and willingly shared her extensive knowledge with me."

At home that evening, Loveday was brimming with excitement. "What was the Queen wearing?"

Arthur thought. "A coat," he said vaguely. "Lilac, I think, like her hat. And lots of pearls."

From then on, he determined to offer the Queen a token of his admiration and his opportunity came almost immediately. 1935 was the year of the Silver Jubilee and although the official celebrations were over by the time of the Russian Art Exhibition, Emanuel Snowman thought it was not too late to mark the occasion.

Arthur wanted to offer the Queen a piece of Fabergé to add to her already extensive collection.

"No," said Snowman, whose royal barometer was exquisitely fine-tuned, "that would be too personal, but a gift to Her Majesty's Chapel of the Savoy could be acceptable. We have a fine Lapis Lazuli cross in the shop you might consider."

Arthur looked at the cross and tried to imagine if the Queen would like it. Then he visited the Chapel. "There's already a silver cross," he told Snowman.

"Trust me," said his new friend, and Arthur did. He bought the cross and sent it to the Queen's Chapel with a note expressing his congratulations on the Jubilee. Then he waited and fantasised about receiving a personal note from the Queen. At the end of July, however, he received a letter from the Chaplain's assistant at the Chapel thanking him profusely for his gift and saying that the Queen had graciously consented to his cross being placed upon the altar. Dr. Derry would arrange with Wartski to have his Lapis cross inserted in the silver one *in situ*.

Immediately following the Belgrave Square exhibition Arthur made up his mind to create a collection that would rival the Royal one. He mentioned this to Emanuel Snowman.

Again, the opportunity to acquire something fabulous occurred almost immediately. The phone rang at The Grange late one Friday night, startling everyone.

"Who can that be ringing up so late?" said Evelyn who was half listening to a play on the wireless. "It must urgent; maybe someone has died."

"More likely somebody cancelling this weekend," said Loveday. "Well, who is going to answer it?"

They all looked at Arthur who was half asleep deep in his armchair with two dogs supine on his lap.

"He's not going," said Evelyn, as the phone went on ringing. "You go, Loveday, please."

But Loveday, who was lying on the floor with her sister and Ailey playing Monopoly, the very newest board game, was on the point of buying Park

Lane, next to Mayfair the most desirable and expensive property of the game. She wasn't going to take her eyes off the board for a second, so she ignored her mother (not something she would do lightly).

"I'll go," said Ailey, getting up. "Don't either of you touch anything while I'm gone." She walked into the hall and picked up the phone while everyone tried to listen. They heard her say "Steeple Aston 204" and after a very brief exchange she came back into the room and said, "It's Mr Snowman for you, Arthur."

"What can he possibly want this late?" said Evelyn, relieved that it wasn't a death or emergency, but irritated that Emanuel Snowman thought it was permissible to telephone so late at night.

Arthur lifted the dogs off his lap onto the floor, heaved himself out of the chair and left the room, closing the door behind him. He was gone for five minutes. On his return, "I have to go to London in the morning," he said.

"But you can't," objected his wife. "We have guests for the weekend, your friends if you remember, you must be here when they arrive. And we have been invited to a garden party in the afternoon."

"Sorry about that," said Arthur, "but something important has come up and I'm sure the Grimshaws won't mind, and I know you can cope with Batters and Binkie," and he winked at Loveday.

"That is not the point," said Evelyn, working herself up. "I'm sure whatever trinket Mr Snowman has to show you can wait until Monday."

"Perhaps," said Arthur, "but I can't, Bet. I shall drive up early and be back in time for lunch."

But he wasn't back for lunch and it wasn't a trinket. When he arrived at Wartski the following morning, after exchanging the usual pleasantries, Emanuel Snowman ushered him downstairs before he could look around the shop.

On a table in the middle of the subterranean room was a single object, a gold egg about five inches tall, on a stand. Arthur stepped close to have a look.

It was breathtaking; carefully lit by Snowman, it blazed with gold guilloche enamel in a starburst pattern, a lattice of diamonds covered the egg and at each intersection was the Romanov Imperial double-headed eagle in gold outlined in black enamel and set with a diamond. On the top was a large diamond set within a circle of ten brilliant diamonds.

"If you look into the big diamond you will see the Tsarina's monogram," said Snowman softly. It was the first time either man had spoken. Arthur peered at the two Russian initials outlined in diamonds.

"Marvellous," he said. Snowman stepped forward and lifted the top of the egg. Inside, a lining of white velvet revealed another object which he lifted out carefully and placed on the table beside the egg. It was a miniature coach. Snowman opened a tiny door revealing a red interior and let down a set of red and gold steps. Arthur felt slightly dizzy. "What is this?" he breathed.

"This is the Coronation Egg," said Snowman. "The Tsarina rode to her coronation in 1897 in this coach," he continued, pointing to the miniature. "You can pick it up and have a look inside."

An hour later the two men were still poring over the treasure. Money had not been mentioned but Arthur knew without question that he must buy the Egg if it was available. He did not think that Snowman would show him something that was not for sale, and he was right. The price, when it was finally mentioned, was not a great surprise. Slightly less than two thousand pounds, Arthur did not hesitate. It was a momentous purchase and Snowman took him to lunch at Simpsons and ordered champagne.

Arthur arrived home somewhat late in the afternoon. He had missed lunch, and the family had left for the garden party, but he had the Coronation Egg in his pocket, and he went immediately to the dining room, followed by dogs, to find a suitable place for it. He would show it off at dinner, and "they would all be so amazed at its beauty that Bet would forget to be cross," he said to the dogs.

In September Arthur bought a Russian gold snuff box he had seen on his first visit for £1550, and in November that same year he acquired another Easter Egg, (though this is now disputed) the Imperial Bay Tree Egg along with eight other items, for £2555. Arthur was now a valued client and Snowman gave him a lilac guilloché enamel Fabergé cigarette case decorated with the Imperial eagles to mark the first year of their friendship. It was engraved *To Arthur E. Bradshaw a man who radiates happiness and charm, Emanuel Snowman 1935*. Over the next few years Arthur would acquire more than forty cigarette cases, some more lavishly decorated in gold, rock crystal, diamonds, and rubies, but this one he kept with him always. By this time Arthur had become Braddie, as he had been amongst his sporting friends in South Africa, and Emanuel Snowman, Snowy. In all, in his first year of collecting Arthur spent almost £7000.

Loveday was thrilled with her birthday bracelet, but Evelyn saw a pattern of visits to London developing. Though she had no idea how much he was spending, she worried as the treasures accumulated. She suggested that Arthur should invite Snowy to The Grange, where she would be able to witness the alchemy and oversee the purchases. She thought her presence might curb his spending, but she was wrong. Arthur jumped at the suggestion and thus began a routine that saw him acquire, thanks to Snowy's visits over the next four years, eight hundred jewels, carvings, boxes, clocks and watches, photo frames, drinking vessels, animals, figures, flowers, cigarette cases and Imperial Eggs.

"Where are you keeping them?" Snowy asked, as Arthur's collection grew ever larger.

"At the moment they are all on tables and the mantelpiece in the dining room, but I think I must have some cabinets made like you have here," he said, waving at the shop fittings.

"There is bound to be a good cabinet maker in Oxford," said Snowy, "what with all the rare books and museum artefacts I'm sure are kept behind glass. I'll come and help you display your treasures if you like."

Arthur nodded. "I'd like that very much," he said, "I will get on with it."

He found a family firm of three generations of cabinet makers on the outskirts of Oxford, and to start with he commissioned three glass-fronted cases, each with four glass shelves. Father and son came to The Grange to measure up. The son's jaw dropped when he saw the jewelled treasures just sitting about on tables. The father hissed at his boy to shut his mouth, then said casually to Arthur, "Got any cats, Sir?"

"No." Arthur smiled, realising what the question implied. "Only a few dachshunds and they can't reach."

"Just as well there's no cats," said the son on the way home as the van lurched over the uneven street paving. "Just imagine what a world of damage they could do in that room."

The doorbell rang and set off a chorus of barking from the entanglement of dachshunds around the sofa. Arthur put down his book and swung his legs onto the floor, trampling on two of the dogs as he made his way across the room, followed by the pack of seven. He stopped briefly beside his wife, who was reading an illustrated paper, and touched her shoulder. Evelyn looked up at him with a slow smile but said nothing, so he turned and left the room. She didn't return to her magazine but laying it aside, she rose and went to the window.

As she suspected, Emanuel Snowman was standing on the terrace. Evelyn sighed. He would have a treasure or two in his pockets that

Arthur would be unable to resist. Where was it all going to end? They would be in the poorhouse if Arthur kept up this pace of collecting. It amounted to a mania in her opinion. Everything that Wartski showed him, he bought. Most of the jewels and precious objects were too rich for her taste. She wore little in the way of jewellery, though she knew that Arthur would give her anything she admired. Although some of the pieces he bought were extravagant and lovely, most to her way of thinking were useless. She watched as Snowy smiled in greeting at her unseen husband and disappeared from her view.

Arthur would take him to the dining room where he now had several glass-fronted cabinets to display his treasured objects, she thought, and the two men would pore over whatever Snowy had brought with him and then find space for it on the shelves. The transaction always concluded with a glass of madeira. Evelyn looked at the clock on the mantlepiece. It was late enough to offer the visitor afternoon tea before he returned to London. She did not want him to linger into the evening when he would have to be offered dinner, and then it would be too late to return on the train to London, so he'd be staying the night. No, thought Evelyn. I will order a substantial tea to be served to the men in the dining room, sandwiches, and cakes. Then, she hoped, Arthur would ask for the car and Snowy would be on his way to the station.

Returning to her chair she wondered how she had overlooked this visit. Snowy always telephoned in advance to make sure of a convenient time and there had been occasions, when Arthur was out and about, when she had been able to ask the butler to intercept him on the doorstep and declare that alas, Mr Bradshaw had forgotten the appointment and was not at home. A small deception, but it might slow what Evelyn saw as an ever-increasing passion for these very expensive and impractical objects.

She acknowledged that Emanuel Snowman was now a friend of Arthur's through their shared interest. As George Villiers had been a friend because of their mutual admiration for each other's gardens, and she thought Dick Wadham was probably in the friend category, though in a different way. They had long conversations, he and Arthur, and Evelyn thought they were not all about gardening. Dick had his own homespun philosophy and she could sometimes tell when an idea of his crept into Arthur's conversation. Her husband was a sociable man, expansive, charming, and generous. He has so many friends, she thought, perhaps hundreds, while she had very few; Ailey her oldest and best. And half a dozen couples, friends of Arthur's, that she had come to know and like. Of his Masonic friends she knew nothing, nor about his sporting chums in South Africa, though they occasionally turned up for a weekend at The Grange. When it came to family, Stewart and Kate were the closest to her husband, after her of course. Evelyn had no doubt that she came first in Arthur's affection.

"You must come and look, Bet." Her reverie interrupted, she turned to see Arthur in the doorway attended by a couple of dogs. "You have to see it." He took her hand and hurried her into the dining room. Emmanuel Snowman put down his cup and rose to his feet, bowing slightly in her direction.

"Good afternoon Mrs Bradshaw," he said, brushing away an imaginary crumb. She smiled and held out her hand.

"How are you, Mr Snowman?" Their formality contrasted with the easy intimacy of the men's relationship and that was the way she wished it to be. Snowy wasn't going to get under her skin with his flattery and baubles. The men stood back from the table to allow Evelyn a proper view. A single spray of lily-of-the-valley made of pearls and diamonds, with a jade leaf and set into a crystal vase, twinkled at her.

"Another one," she said. "How many are there?"

"We don't exactly know," said Snowy, "but is it not exquisite?"

"Yes," said Arthur, "and I want them all. I want a garden." He picked up the flower and, opening a door to one of his cabinets, placed it on a shelf with four others.

"You shall have them," said Snowy. "Whatever we can find."

The two men bent their heads over the treasure, Evelyn already forgotten. She turned and silently left the room.

Evelyn shared her concerns about Arthur's extravagance with Stewart.

"What is it?" she said. "What is he doing? I don't understand his behaviour. There is something urgent about it that really bothers me."

They were walking slowly through the garden, Stewart carrying a basket while Evelyn picked the last of the roses. Autumn was giving way to winter. Three dogs were sitting, watching; they knew this was not a proper walk, but it might turn into something.

Stewart lit his pipe and drew on it thoughtfully. "It's an enchantment," he said finally. "He has found a new friend and a new love." Stewart liked the worldly Emanuel Snowman. "He is under a spell. And he is blissfully happy," he added quickly.

"But he is spending so much money."

"I wouldn't worry about that, Bet." Stewart understood the workings of the brewery and the family finances. "There is more than enough to go round. And the things he is collecting are beautiful, don't you think?"

Evelyn was torn. "Some of them are," she said reluctantly, although they were tainted in her mind with the Revolution and its terrible consequences for the Imperial family. "But I can't help thinking about where they came from." Then, "Am I being a shrew?"

Stewart looked at her kindly. "No, Bet, I can understand your concern, but you don't need to worry."

So far as her emotional response to the Romanov's massacre went, it was a feminine perspective; he knew his wife would think the same way and there was really no answer.

"Time to go in," he said. "It is getting chilly." They turned towards the house, and the dogs rose to follow them.

"I'll keep an eye on Mo's spending," he said.

Evelyn looked at him gratefully. "Thank you," she said.

Arthur returned from London in high spirits. He was almost jiggling with excitement.

"Look, look," he exclaimed, taking something from his bag and placing it on the table. Evelyn looked and saw a small box, gold and glittery with diamonds.

"Oh! how lovely." She couldn't help herself. And it was indeed lovely. Oblong gold, with yellow enamel, the top criss-crossed and marked with diamonds, Imperial Eagles in the diamond shapes with a circle of diamonds in the centre and the initials N II. "What is it?"

Arthur took a deep breath. "It is a coronation box presented to Tsar Nicholas by the Tsarina Alexandra in 1897. By Fabergé," he added, almost unnecessarily. Evelyn nodded. Arthur picked up the box and held it out to her. "Open it," he said.

She shook her head and put her hands behind her back. The tragedy of the Romanovs and their bloody end moved her to tears and she wanted nothing to do with their personal treasures. But Arthur kept buying them. She had lost count of the number of boxes he had collected.

"How much did it cost?" she murmured, turning away, but he didn't hear her. He was already opening a display cabinet and moving things around on a shelf to find a place for the box. Then he seemed to change his mind and closed the door, slipping the box into his pocket.

"I think I will keep it on my desk for a while to get to know it properly."

***

Arthur filled his pockets with dog biscuits and opened the back door. The chill air flowed in off the lawn and a cat's tail of fog curled around his legs. He shivered and lit a cigarette then, overtaken by a fit of coughing, he clutched at the door lintel and cursed. He knew he must see his doctor about the bronchitis that had plagued him all winter. Unable to get to South Africa, he had suffered, but now it was spring, and it should be clearing up. Bet had been nagging. They would go abroad next year.

The dogs scuttled past down the steps and ran, barking at imaginary rabbits, across the garden where some myriad cobwebs hung, flashing diamonds in the weak glow of a low sun that filtered through the trees. The storm that lashed the house overnight had left a few fallen limbs in the park. The woodcutters would see to the clearing up.

Calling to the dogs, he set off down the steps with his slightly lumbering walk forever braced against the ocean swells, and into garden to check the damage. The bowling green, newly prepared, was of particular concern as a tournament had been arranged for the weekend. Dick was already inspecting the lawn beside the greenhouse. The men greeted each other and walked carefully on the grass. It was spongy and wet, and a few twigs lay at the far border but otherwise Arthur couldn't see any damage.

"This'll dry out by Saturday," said Dick. "That is if we don't have more rain." Arthur nodded. The dogs raced across the green and disappeared into the undergrowth, hunting invisible quarry. Dick bent to remove some timber. "I'll mow it again on Saturday, early."

Arthur looked up at the sky. A black cloud of starlings wheeled overhead, pulsating to their own mysterious rhythm, circling, swooping and curving joyfully in unison. A murmuration, Arthur said to himself, pleased that he remembered. The two men stood and watched the birds in silence.

"I'll have a look at the park before it gets dark," he said and, calling the dogs, he set off, surrounded by his retinue.

"Woodcutters have been sent for," Dick called after him. Arthur waved. His head gardener and the six under-gardeners did a splendid job maintaining The Grange much as his father had left it, but in the twenty-five years since Richard's death there had been some additions, and Arthur was particularly proud of the restoration of the bowling green. The Steeple Aston bowling club comprised thirty-five members who enjoyed almost unlimited access, and there were frequent tournaments with the neighbouring villages.

Snow had fallen overnight. Arthur stood at the window looking out over the dazzling white garden. He shivered. Another winter when he hadn't been able to get to South Africa. He watched a solitary jackdaw alight on a branch, shaking off a small shower of glittering crystals. Hands clasped behind his back, he rocked on his heels. A handsome red fox crossed his vision, making tracks across the snow, dragging his brush, ears pricked, mouth open, scenting the air. They are the first and last footprints of that fox, on this day, on my lawn, for no fox steps on the same patch of snow twice, Arthur thought suddenly, paraphrasing Heraclites.

He felt a wave of emotion, an intimation of the passing of time, but also of everlastingness; that strange conflict which can give rise to a momentary feeling of oneness with the universe. The fox stopped midway, one paw raised, listening for something. A dachshund joined Arthur at the window, noticed the fox and instantly set up a mad barking and scrabbling at the glass. The fox flattened his ears and moved quickly to the far side of the lawn, slid under a barred gate and was gone into the trees.

Arthur wanted to open the window and shout after him "Go fox, go and enjoy your life of freedom. The Bicester will get you in the end." But he didn't. He patted the dog and feeling in his pockets for a cigarette, turned back into the room where his latest treasure was waiting on a small table. It was an Imperial Easter Egg and it, too, was glittering, but with eternal elements: rubies, emeralds and the biggest yellow diamond Arthur had ever seen. "This one is unique," Snowy had said on the telephone the week before. "You must see it. Shall I bring it?"

"No," said Arthur. "I will come to London."

"This was a special gift from Alexandra to Nicholas during the Tercentenary celebrations in 1913," Snowy announced, when both men were standing, looking at the extraordinary creation. He waited while Arthur absorbed the information. "It has similarities to an Egg known as the Alexander the Third Equestrian Egg. Both have a latticed canopy set with jewels and fringed, and both contain an equestrian statue of a Tsar."

"Where is the other one?" asked Arthur.

"In the Kremlin, and likely to remain there forever," was the reply. "There are some things that the Russian government probably will never sell."

Now in his dining room, Arthur contemplated the treasure before him. On one side was a portrait of the Tsarina Alexandra surrounded by brilliant diamonds, and on the other was the astonishing canary diamond. Arthur had seen yellow diamonds in South Africa in the Cullinan Premier mine sorting room, but none as deep in colour or as brilliant. Was it this, or proximity to the pale green enamel that worked the Fabergé magic? He turned the egg and the rubies in the canopy winked. Then he held his breath and pressed the cabochon emerald set in the top. The egg divided silently into two halves, revealing a silver model of Nicholas II on horseback holding a flag. The horse stood on cobblestones outlined in almost invisible diamonds. He tried to imagine the Tsar's reaction the first time he opened his egg. It had always been the other way around. He gave the Easter gifts to the Tsarina. Now she had given this one, the first and only egg, to him. It must have a special place, Arthur said to the dachshund. The dog followed him into the dining room where he opened the door to the cabinet that already held the Coronation Egg and started moving objects around to accommodate his newest treasure.

"Starlight, star bright, first star I see tonight." Eira was leaning out of the open window of the dining room, gazing at the pale twinkle of the Evening Star. It was a balmy spring evening.

Loveday entered the room jingling the keys to her new car, a present for her twenty-first birthday, one of the first Jaguars, an SS 100 and incredibly smart. She joined Eira at the window.

"Wish I may, wish I might, have the wish I wish tonight," Eira chanted and Loveday chimed in. "Make a wish!" The girls scrunched their eyes tight shut and wished.

"What did you wish for?" Stewart had entered the room and was looking over their shoulders. "Look, Venus," he said.

"We know," chorused the girls.

Then, "I can't tell you my wish or it won't come true," said Eira.

"I know what it is," said Loveday. "It's the same thing we both wish for all the time, that Dad's cough would get better."

Stewart looked serious. "Yes, we all wish for that," he said. "Your father needs to get away to somewhere warm, that would help a lot."

"It would also help if he stopped smoking so much!" Ailey had come in looking for Eira. They all turned to look at her. "Your mother wants you to help her sort out some clothes to go to the Almshouses," she said. Eira rolled her eyes, but she hopped down off the window seat and left the room. They heard her pounding up the stairs.

"Is it just smoking?" Stewart asked. "We all smoke, and yes, I know

Bob died of lung cancer amongst other ailments, but nobody coughs like Mo."

Ailey, who did not smoke, shrugged. "I think he smokes too much. I know that the medical profession thinks there is no harm in it, and some doctors even recommend certain brands, but I wonder about that sort of advertising. I hear that the village doctor gets cartons of free cigarettes from a certain company, and they expect him to extol the virtues of that brand."

"You are an old sceptic," said Stewart, but privately he wondered if there might be some truth in what Ailey was saying. Still, it was most unlikely that Mo would heed any appeal to give up the habit. He knew that Bet had tried to talk to him about smoking less, but to no avail.

He and Ailey stood by the window talking quietly while Loveday wandered around the room, humming. and looking at the ornaments in the display cases. She particularly liked the pansies and the lilies of the valley, so realistically rendered in their crystal vases seemingly half filled with water. No one was allowed to touch them unless Arthur was in the room and said that they could. Bobby had once asked if he could take the Russian figures out of their case, but Arthur had made it quite clear that they were not toys. He did, however, show Bobby the figures one by one, explaining what each one represented.

"What are you doing this summer?" Stewart asked Loveday as she finished her tour of the collection and joined them at the window.

Ailey put her arm around Loveday's shoulders. "This talented beauty is playing her oboe in the Glyndebourne orchestra," she said.

"That sounds like hard work," said Stewart, who had no ear for music. "How did it happen?"

"Well Mum and Dad are friends with the Christies, and when my music teacher suggested I was competent enough to join a small orchestra, I was invited. I only had to learn the one score, and it's the best fun; we camp in a field beside the house, in caravans, we play in the afternoon and evening. It's so glamorous. All the guests are in evening dress and there are lots of jewels." Loveday was known for liking jewels.

"What are you playing?" Ailey asked.

"Mozart", said Loveday, "'The Marriage of Figaro'." Stewart looked blank. "It's really famous, Uncle Cuckoo," she insisted.

He laughed. "Good for you," he said.

"Let's have some popular music," said Stewart, when Eira reappeared. "What shall we play?"

The girls moved to the gramophone and started searching through the stack of records on the table. Arthur had bought the gramophone when his hero Sir Edward Elgar opened the shop in Oxford Street in 1921; the combination of the composer and the HMV Jack Russell was irresistible. Most of the records were Elgar; he loved the Pomp and Circumstance marches, Nimrod made him weep, and the mysterious cantata 'Caractacus', dedicated to Queen Victoria, contained his favourite song.

"Here's something," said Loveday, pulling The Mikado out of the pile. "We can sing along to this," and she put the disc on the turntable and wound the handle. In a moment the girls were happily twirling and trilling 'Three Little Maids from School Are We,' with Ailey soon joining in.

How young they are, thought Stewart, and how blissfully unaware of what life could deal out. He leaned against the wall watching the sky darken and more stars appear, and he had a fleeting moment of regret that he and Clarie had never had children. Arthur was lucky to have his Bobby, the last of the Bradshaws. As for the rest, there were girls; these two girls and Harry's daughter, Elinor. The rest were Sales. Five brothers, and only one of us produces a son, and if anything happens to him, it's the end of the family name after how many hundred years? (He had, for a moment, forgotten his cousin Hugh in the army, and his son

Stuart). Then he shook himself; morbid thoughts, no doubt engendered by talking of Arthur's health, were not good. He closed the window, crossed the room, and joined in the dancing.

The last voyage abroad for the family took place in 1937. Britain was still simmering in the aftermath of Edward VIII's abdication, followed by the coronation of George VI and Queen Elizabeth in May. This took some of the heat out of the situation as, with their two small princesses, they looked like a devoted and stable family, the opposite of the playboy prince who had given up his throne for a woman the public would not tolerate. By the time the (by then) Duke of Windsor married Wallis Simpson in June in the South of France, Arthur with Evelyn and daughters Eira and Loveday were aboard the *Njassa* en route to Cape Town.

Evelyn pushed aside her fear of the ocean by reading Agatha Christie's latest mystery Death on the Nile and made the round trip via Port Said, Lisbon, Mombasa, Beira, and Dar es Salaam in relatively more comfort than she had anticipated. It was probably her first and only visit to the country where her husband had spent so much of his time away from her in the early days.

There was a knock on the door. Eira opened to find her father. "What is it Daddy?" He looked at her tangled hair and rumpled nightgown. It had been another late night for the girls.

"Getting up time," he said.

"But it's so early!" she protested.

He looked past her into the cabin at Loveday's bunk. "Show a leg," he said, and heard a muffled groan as she pulled the blanket over her head. "We have rounded the corner and I want you both on deck to see Cape Town at sunrise. It's a lovely sight and really, it's what we have come all this way to see. Your mother is dressed and ready," he added, as if that would be an incentive. The ship rolled and Eira clutched at the door, while Arthur barely moved. Then he turned and set off down the passage. "You'll need something warm," he called over his shoulder, "and don't be long."

For the girls, the voyage was exciting and liberating; there were deck games during the day and handsome young crew to dance with at night. They were having a lot of fun.

"We'd better get up," said Eira. "We don't want him in a bad mood, or he might send us to bed early." Eira had plans.

The girls arrived on deck ten minutes later, wrapped in coats. Loveday was wearing sunglasses, while Eira blinked in the sharp early light. Arthur and Evelyn were standing at the rail looking at Cape Town. Evelyn had a camera in her hand, but the city was too far away and not yet lit by the sun. "How long do we have here, Mo?"

"Just a day," he said, "but long enough for me to show you a few of my favourite places. We will lunch at the Lord Nelson Hotel, then take the cable car up Table Mountain for the truly spectacular view. We'll finish off with tea at the Olympic Sports Club."

And so they did. The members of the Olympic, apprised of Arthur's impending visit with his family, made a big effort to round up anyone who remembered him, and laid on a lavish afternoon tea. An elderly member approached Arthur. "I remember you Bradshaw," he trumpeted, "good sport, gave us a trophy didn't you? Is this the family?" he turned towards Loveday and Eira. "I thought there was a boy."

"There is," said Arthur, "but he is still at school."

The old man thought for a moment, then turned and lumbered towards Evelyn. He peered at her, and Arthur, who had followed, arrived just in time to hear him say, "So Mrs. Bradshaw, you're the reason he stopped coming here. All that time, regular as clockwork, he came every year for six months, then suddenly, he got married and we haven't seen him for over twenty years."

"There was a war as well," said Arthur mildly, steering his wife away from any further interrogation.

Happily, at that moment the wives of the members, determined to make a fuss of Evelyn, gathered around and presented her with a huge bunch of flowers which, though surprised and flattered, she didn't quite know what to do with. "I felt like minor royalty," she said to Arthur later, as their cabin steward fetched a vase.

The family returned to the ship happy. Arthur was elated that the day had gone so well, Evelyn was flattered by the attention, and the girls were looking forward to an evening of flirting and dancing.

There are few photographs taken on this voyage.

On their return to England Emanuel Snowman suggested they accompany him to the International Exposition of Art and Technology in Modern Life, in Paris. He and his wife were making a return visit, such were the fascinating displays. This exhibition, which ran from May to November in 1937, contained pavilions from 45 countries displaying such wonders as Picasso's *Guernica* from Spain, a 28-foot-high sculpture of a buffalo from Canada, while the German pavilion, designed by Albert Speer, displayed the prescient swastika on its tower, and positioned outside the entrance was a sculpture of two enormous male nudes holding hands. The French pavilion was a tent designed by Le Corbusier while Italy, bypassing to some extent the 'moderne' of the exhibition's title, chose to show Murano glass chandeliers, a central courtyard of green grass and red flowers, and to serve spaghetti at the terrace restaurant.

The English pavilion was a modest affair, criticised by some for eschewing modernity and focussing on traditional crafts instead of projecting national strength. The main item of interest was a large photograph of Neville Chamberlain fishing.

Arthur and Evelyn journeyed to Paris where they spent a few days. Arthur was fascinated by some of the exhibits, but Evelyn found the overt politics of Nazi Germany and the Soviet Union thoroughly distasteful and said so.

Arthur smiled. "David Mitford would agree with you," he said. He shouted his hatred of Germany loud and long, though astonishingly, in 1939 he and Sydney were persuaded to accompany their daughters Unity – just a year older than Loveday – and Diana to Germany, where they attended the Nuremburg rally and met Hitler.

Both were won over by his superficial charm, but the moment war was declared David recanted, and once again became violently anti-German.

In Paris now, and more of interest to her, were the bookstalls on the Left Bank and window shopping in the rue de Rivoli with her friend Blanche Deval, who had come to Paris to see the exhibition and spend time with her. They dined with Emanuel and Harriet Snowman, Jack Callum, the second in command at Wartski, and Blanche, at a restaurant labelled by Evelyn as Le Roi George but more likely was that of the Georges Cinq Hotel.

Arthur and Snowy spent a morning at an establishment famous for antique jewellery where they both bought watches. Arthur was delighted to find a gold Royalist watch by Breguet dated 1790 with a portrait of the Royal Family inside, and a blue enamel clock set with pearls and a diamond fleur-de-lis. Temptation, it seemed, was everywhere. It was something of a relief for Evelyn to return to The Grange.

1938

"There should be an inventory." Emanuel Snowman was showing Arthur a small collection of carved animals in the shop. "You have hundreds of treasures now. It is a unique collection and it must be noted down in case, God forbid, anything should happen."

Arthur smiled modestly. "I did start making quite a long list, but it really should be done professionally, don't you think?" He picked up a small jade elephant. "This is exquisite. I have a few elephants now. I often wonder what is so appealing about them."

"It's the craftmanship," said Snowy. "Will you take it?" The question was rhetorical. There was nothing he had ever shown Arthur that had been refused. He was confident all the animals would shortly be on their way to Steeple Aston.

Arthur arranged a few into a circle. "I wish I had more space in my cabinets so they could be arranged in groups."

"I'm sure we can organise the cabinets differently at the time of cataloguing."

"Will you come?"

"Yes, of course, but first I will send two people from the shop to compile the inventory. It may take a few days. Is there somewhere they can put up in the village?"

"Don't be silly," said Arthur, "they must stay at The Grange. There is plenty of room. Shall we say next week?"

Evelyn was not overly pleased at the thought of an invasion of shop assistants whom she didn't know, but she accepted the logic of cataloguing Arthur's collection and said nothing.

The two young men from the shop gazed in silent awe at the cabinets in the dining room. They knew, of course, that Arthur was one of their most important clients but had no idea until that moment of the extent of his collection.

"God," said one under his breath, "where do we start?"

"I think," said his companion, "we will do it in categories even though they are randomly displayed. We will take all the cigarette cases out, for example, put them on this table, note them all then put them back. And wait for Mr. Snowdon to come and rearrange things." He opened a large ledger and handed his assistant a pair of white cotton gloves. "Here, you take them out and I'll write them down."

That was Monday. Evelyn realised that it would be best if they arranged to have their meals in the kitchen while this was going on. The dining table was half covered with ornaments as the two men bent industriously over their task. They could hardly clear it all away three times a day for meals or she feared they would be there for a month. The young men, who had nice manners, were invited to join the family for meals. They made a hasty breakfast and got down to their task by nine. At lunch the girls would ask them questions, and in the evening they went off to the Red Lion for a meal. Often Loveday and Eira went with them and came home giggling.

Occasionally the girls peeped around the door to see what the men were doing but had been strictly forbidden by Evelyn to interrupt. She did not want them staying any longer than necessary. Arthur wandered in and out to see how it was progressing and of course, was fascinated to see his objects arranged in categories. He wondered if they should return to the cabinets the same way but thought he would let Snowy decide.

On Friday morning the men finished. There were over 800 items listed and even Arthur was amazed. They thanked Arthur and Evelyn for their hospitality and left for London. Snowy arrived in the afternoon and he and Arthur spent the weekend rearranging everything.

"It will take some time to type it all up," said Snowy, "and we will bind it in a folder. Would you like the family crest on the front page?" There was a framed crest hanging in the study.

"Is that a bit showy off?"

"I don't think so. This collection is a family heirloom and as such deserves to have a formal family stamp on it. What do you think, Mrs. Bradshaw?" Snowy, smiling, turned to Evelyn.

Evelyn demurred. "Whatever Arthur thinks is best." Privately she hoped that the inventory would draw a line under Arthur's buying sprees. This might be the end of it.

1939

Although longing to get away from the winter, Arthur was racked with his cough and so ill that by December 1938, travel was out of the question.

"Best not," said his doctor. "You need constant medical attention."

"I would be better in a warmer climate," Arthur argued.

"Perhaps," came the rejoinder, "but you must get there, and it's the travelling that I am worried about."

Arthur fumed, but was too weak to protest much, so Christmas was spent, somewhat miserably, at home. Evelyn invited all the family. Most came and made comforting noises about how he would feel better when the spring came, but Arthur was not convinced. Stewart, whose wife was very ill, did not come but stayed in Brighton, though what good the sea air would do her at this time of year nobody was quite certain. Clarie died just after Christmas, adding another layer of gloom to the gathering.

The roads were so icy as to be impassable and none of the family was able to attend her funeral. Evelyn wrote, and The Grange sent a wreath. It had been a comfortable union but without children. Stewart came to The Grange immediately following the funeral. He made a valiant effort to be cheerful, but mostly he sat and stared out at the snow-covered landscape, constantly running his hands over his hair. One or two dogs kept him company. Arthur patted his shoulder in passing and handed him a whisky in the evening.

"I expect Stewart will be lonely," said Evelyn said to Kate. They were talking in low voices in the scullery while sorting table silver as the 'boots' was busy elsewhere. Outside it was snowing.

"Oh, I don't know," said Kate, who was polishing a candlestick, determined to make New Year's Eve as festive as possible. "Stewart has a multitude of friends in the racing world, and then there are all those rowers. I expect they will rally. He will be occupied. He might even marry again – he is so gregarious."

"Not so soon!" exclaimed Evelyn, slightly horrified at her sister-in-law's apparently callous dismissal of the barely deceased wife.

Kate smiled. "I'm not sentimental like you, Bet," she said, "and I don't think Stewart will like being alone."

Worse was to come; Arthur's gardener and friend, Dick, died. He had been ill for some time, and Arthur had watched his decline with alarm as it seemingly mirrored his own. Heavily muffled, in December, he insisted on visiting Dick in his Oxford hospital and came home deeply saddened. "I won't see him again," he said to Evelyn.

On Christmas Eve, Evelyn donned her boots and a fur coat and visited the Wadham's cottage, with the annual Box, to express the family's concern for Dick's health.

"Not much hope now," said his daughter, one of three sitting around the fire while the three sons stood uncomfortably in the kitchen.

Evelyn took her hand. "If there is anything we can do, let us know please," she said.

Dick died four days later, and his funeral was held in Steeple Aston on 5th January. Arthur fretted, as he was strongly advised by his doctor not to attend owing to the bitter cold, but John made the effort to come, as did Stewart, and they went with Evelyn and the children to the church to farewell their most faithful retainer.

"There was a good crowd," Evelyn said afterwards. "People from horticultural societies and bowling clubs, as you'd expect."

"I should have been there," said Arthur, "he was my friend."

Over the next few months Arthur slowly declined. By midsummer he was very ill. "Can you do something?" he asked his doctor.

"I think we should put you in hospital and have a closer look at your lungs," said the good man. "Perhaps one of them should come out."

"An operation?"

"Yes. I will make the arrangements."

Though horrified at the prospect, when the time came, he went quietly into the University College Hospital in London and one hopelessly diseased lung was removed. The *Banbury Advertiser* recorded the event on Arthur's return to Steeple Aston, reporting that he was "still very ill."

On his return to The Grange, Emanuel Snowman sent a silver salver as a cheering up present. It was engraved *To Mr and Mrs A E Bradshaw with affection and every good wish from Harriette and Snowy June 17th, 1939.* Arthur smiled at the inscription, the formality between Snowy and Bet still existed.

A register of England and Wales taken in 1939 also recorded the fact, strangely, that "the householder was seriously ill." Loveday and her fiancé Bryan Burleston, a Lloyd's broker, were staying at The Grange at the time and, seeing the situation, she took on the role of nursing her father. However, before long it was necessary for Arthur to have round-the-clock attention, two state registered nurses, Muriel Harewood and Dorothy Knight, moved into The Grange to attend to him in shifts.

I should feel better, thought Arthur, and he said as much to Evelyn, but she knew what he did not: both his lungs were diseased, and they had simply taken the worse one.

"Don't tell him," said the doctor, and she agreed, but privately she thought that Arthur already knew his days were numbered.

From then on it was about making Arthur comfortable. For a while he managed a short excursion daily with the dogs into the garden, consulted with the new head gardener about the likelihood of a bowling tournament and, despite Evelyn's protests, insisted that Snowy visit him.

Emanuel Snowman came and brought one or two little objects to show Arthur but tactfully did not pressure him to buy anything. The two men spent time in the dining room, taking Arthur's favourite objects from the cabinets to examine and repeat their history. This was his favourite distraction. Evelyn left them alone, just sending in tea and cakes. Seeing Snowy's genuine concern for Arthur and the friendship between them, she warmed to him, once or twice insisting that he stayed for the night. He knew without being told that Arthur was dying and realised the unspoken agreement that his illness was not to be mentioned either at The Grange or in London.

Meanwhile the rumbling preludes to the Second World War had been taking place in Europe, but The Grange remained isolated, with only Bobby and Bryan Burleston, in the Royal Navy but not in uniform at The Grange, having any involvement. In 1939, as a midshipman, Bobby was training with the Royal Navy Fleet Air Arm, 826 Squadron at Gravesend. He went on to command the squadron and became one of the great wartime aces.

It was Bobby who noticed and said something. Home for a weekend from his air force training, he had been clowning around with the dogs while his mother took photos. It was hot, and Arthur removed his jacket.

"You've lost weight, Dad."

"I know," said Arthur. "Your mother is trying to feed me up but look how thin she is." He ran a hand over his hair, lit a cigarette, and coughed. "I am going inside. It's too hot."

"Just one more photo," pleaded Evelyn. Arthur paused at the foot of the steps and turned towards her. Bobby stood beside him and struck a pose, hand on hip and his head on one side. The camera clicked, and

Arthur turned and climbed the steps.

"Is Dad all right? He seems tired as well as rather thin."

Evelyn was deliberately vague. "I think so," she said. "It's the heat and he has been coughing more lately. Perhaps he should see a doctor." She swung the camera up to Bobby's shoulder and took another photo just of his face.

"Oh! Stop it, Mum," he said, laughing. "You're a menace with that thing."

On 1st September, Hitler invaded Poland. The government declared mobilisation of the armed forces, and on 3rd, Prime Minister Neville Chamberlain announced on the BBC that the final ultimatum for Germany to withdraw its troops from Poland had expired, and consequently Britain was at war with Germany. The news was kept from Arthur, but he had heard the wireless reports despite the best efforts of Evelyn, Loveday, and his nurses. Proud as he was of his only son and his enthusiasm for flying, he greatly feared for him in the coming conflict.

John and Stewart stood at the window. "It won't be long," said John, looking over the lawn to where Arthur and Evelyn sat.

"He keeps asking for Kate," said Stewart. "What should we tell him?" Rolly, their dearly loved brother-in-law, had died two days before and Kate had arranged the funeral for the following day.

"Nothing," said John. "She won't be coming, and he soon forgets he's asked the question. Now the morphine is taking hold, his mind is wandering."

"I must go to Rolly's funeral," said Stewart. "We cannot leave Katy to the mercy of her mad brother-in-law. She must have family support, so I'll leave first thing in the morning."

John nodded. "Yes, you should go whatever happens here," he said.

Loveday came quietly into the room and stood beside them. John put his arm around her, and she leaned against him. Together, the three stood in silence.

The late October sun slanted across the lawn. It was evening, and a golden autumn glow bathed the garden, deep shadows hiding the late roses. Dogs lay asleep around Arthur, recumbent in his wife's Bath chair, gazing at the hedge as if expecting Dick to come ambling around the corner. He was now too ill to walk. His lilac enamel cigarette case lay unopened on his lap; the urge to smoke having finally left him. Must be near the end, he thought wryly, and a smile started before a racking cough took over and left him gasping and in pain. Evelyn moved to his side and took his hand without speaking. Together they watched the evening encircle the garden.

"What are you thinking, Bet?" He was whispering now.

She smiled. "I was thinking of that morning at the station when you asked me to marry you."

Arthur paused. "I shouldn't have gone off to Africa then," he said. "Selfish. Forgive."

Evelyn bent and kissed the top of his head.

"Time to go in," she said. It was both a question and suggestion. Arthur nodded. She raised her hand towards the house, and a moment later Stewart and John crossed the lawn and the three of them stood beside Arthur, looking at the evening light. It might be the last time, thought Stewart, who had been watching his brother die for months, but it was impossible to be entirely sad in the face of such beauty.

The men turned the chair around, and the dogs stirred and rose to their feet to follow. Arthur was wheeled inside. Passing the door to the dining room he held up his hand to halt the progress.

"What is it dear?" said Evelyn.

"Dog," said Arthur.

Evelyn nodded, and the men coaxed the wicker chair through the door and alongside the cabinets until Arthur indicated stop. Evelyn opened the door and Arthur reached in to a shelf where over a hundred small carved animals were displayed. His hand hovered for some moments, then he chose one and as Evelyn closed the door.

The men wheeled Arthur out and down the passage to where his bedroom had been set up on the ground floor. He lay exhausted, looking through the window as the light faded and the garden turned to shades of grey. The dogs clustered around his bed, a couple whimpering until Stewart picked them up and put them beside him, where they settled immediately.

"Can I get you anything?" Evelyn said softly. Arthur shook his head. He looked up at her and she reached for his free hand. They smiled at each other and she settled in a chair beside the bed as Stewart and John left the room.

"See you tomorrow, old boy," said Stewart from the door.

Arthur coughed. "I suppose so," he whispered, "but I don't think I will be going outside."

Loveday and the nurse slipped quietly in, reattached the drip, then Loveday sat on the other side of the bed to wait. Arthur died just before dawn. Evelyn and Loveday were by his side; the dogs surrounded his bed. His cigarette case lay on the bedside table and in his hand was a small jade Fabergé carving of a dachshund.

The Collection

Collecting has its roots in the hunting and gathering activities that were once necessary for human survival. The collecting hobby of today is a modern descendant of the "cabinet of curiosities," which was common among scholars with the means and opportunities to acquire unusual items from the 16th century onwards. People collect anything and everything; stamps, butterflies, dolls, toys, autographs, postcards, Toby jugs, teapots, books, china shoes, miniature houses, antique glass, sharp objects, art Deco, vintage cars and, in the case of Napoleon, countries. The list is endless, but it is great jewels that have always epitomised beauty, love, romance, danger, and mystery– the Hope diamond and La Pelegrina being famous examples of a cursed jewel that continues to fascinate.

Who then is a collector?

For people who feel strongly about a special time in their lives, collections are emotional; the objects allow them to keep hold of the past, while continuing to live in the present. Then there are those for whom collecting is all about the hunt, the thrill of the chase. For them it is a quest, a lifelong pursuit which can never be completed. Collecting may also provide psychological security by filling a part of the self that one feels is missing. Collectors arrange, organise, and present their objects to the world to be admired. The monetary value is vitally important to some and irrelevant to others.

Hoarders, on the other hand, simply collect compulsively without any thought of order or display; the people who fill their houses with old newspapers is a classic example, or the old lady with twenty-seven cats shut in her kitchen. The hoard can take over the living space; the life of the hoarder leads to health hazards and limited space for daily life functions such as cooking, and not unnaturally having adverse effects on family members. Hoarding is common amongst people who suffer depression or anxiety. Compulsive hoarders may be aware that their behaviour is irrational, but the emotional attachment to the hoarded objects far outweighs any motive to discard the items.

Then there is the person who pays a professional thief to steal, say a Picasso, to be squirreled away and gloated over in a basement where nobody will ever see it. This is in a different category altogether and is not relevant here.

In Arthur's case, what might explain his urge to collect? More than an urge, it was an almost manic desire to accumulate treasures. As a Victorian child, Arthur would have been encouraged to collect stamps, certainly to go on nature rambles to sharpen his observation and collect birds' eggs or pin butterflies – though there is no evidence for this. He was fascinated by his father's collection of African souvenirs, shields, and spears, which were still hanging in the downstairs hall at The Grange when his grandchildren stayed there after the war. But why Fabergé? It is a mystery that the family is at a loss to explain. The time spent with the Cullinans in South Africa in his youth might have taught him about diamonds, and certainly in the small inventory of his personal jewellery, some 34 items, the majority contain diamonds. Interestingly, in nearly all the photos of Evelyn she wears no jewellery, and in only two does she wear any at all; a large pearl pendant in her portrait photo and a pearl chain in a photo taken in a Paris nightclub. Neither of these appears in Arthur's inventory.

If one could make a case for an inherited trait then it is easy to trace Arthur's collecting to his great-great grandfather, Isaac Walker, whose substantial collection of mineral specimens is now in the

Natural History Museum in South Kensington. If that is too much of a stretch, then the urge to possess multiples of such things as cars and dogs was obviously manifest in Arthur early on.

However, once he started on objects, he did not stop at a few choice ornaments, or even a hundred. For him, too much was barely enough. And it wasn't just Fabergé; Arthur bought French, English and German items: watches, clocks, coins, seals, paper knives, vases, photo frames, decanters, plates and glasses; scent bottles, silver, and jewellery in the form of diamond rings and brooches, cufflinks, cameos, crosses and strings of pearls. Of the Russian items, amongst other things there were thirty-eight flower studies, forty-five cigarette cases, ninety-one boxes and an amazing two hundred and fifty-five carved animals and birds. Kovsh. The complete set of twelve carved Russian figures. And three Easter Eggs.

The 1938 inventory was a substantial pile of paper, numbering fifty pages, listing over eight hundred items. A collection of jewels and objets d'art, that might have been the life's work of one man. But it was not Arthur's life's work as only a tiny part of his life, the last four years, had been devoted to amassing the treasures listed. If he had not died at sixty, how much more might he have added to his bewildering collection?

His wife Evelyn had feared his passion would lead them to bankruptcy, but when Arthur's probate was declared he left sixty-two thousand pounds, mostly in Taylor Walker debenture shares and ordinary stock, divided between her and his brother Stewart. Evelyn, thus provided for, lived on at The Grange until her death in 1950. After Arthur's death she sent all but four pieces of Fabergé table silver back to Wartski for sale.

After her death the family sold The Grange and her silver went to auction where the most expensive piece, a large Fabergé silver gilt Kovsh crowned with eagles, was sold to Prince Vladimir Galitzine for 205 pounds, thereby returning to the family who had originally commissioned it.

Somewhat astonishingly, no one in the village of Steeple Aston was aware of Arthur's collection. The family, too, were somewhat vague in their recollections. Arthur was well known for his philanthropy, his involvement with local affairs such as the school, the bowling club, the agricultural events, and his dogs and cars were highly visible and frequently photographed, but the vast collection of Fabergé and others was virtually unknown to outsiders, and there is a single photo of a glass case in the dining room with some figures. Rather than show off his treasures he revelled in them in private, his almost insatiable desire to possess objects of rarity and beauty and to keep them secret, putting him in a borderline category of hoarder.

Among the most collectible objects of the jeweller's art are boxes: snuff boxes, patch boxes, pill boxes, decorative boxes, cigarette and cigar boxes in various designs and every material from gold and enamel to silver, jade, crystal, almost anything that could be carved. Leaving aside cigarette cases and cigar boxes, of which he had a great many, Arthur owned ninety-one other boxes, three of which are described as "gold, gold and enamel with N11 on lid in diamonds by Fabergé" but one goes further and is described as "Yellow Enamel and Gold Box with black enamel double Eagles, set Diamonds, superimposed, and diamond N11 and Crown on lid." This is listed as the Coronation Box in the inventory of Arthur's collection.

The Link of Times Foundation, Fabergé Museum of St. Peterburg.

The Coronation Box (1897)

A diamond-set, enamelled, two-colour gold Imperial presentation snuff box, appliqued with a deep gold hued enamel over guilloché sunburst patterns accented by Imperial eagles and defined by a gold chased trellis set with diamonds. At the centre of the box is a diamond-set monogram of Tsar Nicholas 11 against an oval panel enamelled white with a diamond-set border – signed Fabergé, initials of workmaster August Holmstrom, assay mark of St. Petersburg, length 3 ¾ inches (9.5 cm).

Believed to have been presented by tradition to Tsar Nicholas 11 by Tsarina Alexandra Feodorovna, 1897; however, a recently discovered invoice* now suggests that it was gift to the Chief of the Military Chancellery of the Austrian Emperor Franz Joseph 1, Lieutenant-General Baron Arthur von Bolfras, following the Emperor's visit to St. Petersburg in 1897. So, in fact it was a Presentation box.

Provenance: Herr Bomm, Vienna; Sidney Hill, Berry-Hill Galleries, London and New York; Arthur E. Bradshaw; Lansdell K. Christie, Long Island, New York; the Forbes Magazine Collection, New York.

In 2004 purchased privately by Viktor Vekselberg prior to sale as part of a collection of nine Imperial Easter Eggs from the Forbes Magazine Collection and returned to his Link of Times Collection in the Fabergé Museum in St. Petersburg.

*Ulla Tillander-Godenhielm (2005) *The Russian Imperial Awards*

The Link of Times Foundation, Fabergé Museum of St. Petersburg.

The Coronation Egg (1897)

This egg is one of Fabergé's most recognizable pieces and is a technical zenith in his long and distinguished career. It commemorates the coronation of Nicholas II and Alexandra Feodorovna in Moscow's Uspenski Cathedral, May 26, 1896.

The superb red gold egg, translucent lime-yellow on a guilloche sunburst field, is enclosed by a green-gold laurel leaf trellis-work cage, mounted at each intersection by a yellow-gold Imperial double-headed eagle, enamelled opaque black and set with a diamond. A large portrait diamond is set at the top of the egg, surrounded by a cluster of ten brilliant diamonds. Through the top of this stone the monogram of the Tsarina can be seen, the crowned A in rose-cut diamonds and the Russian F in cabochon rubies set in an opaque enamel plaque.

The concealed surprise is an exact replica of the Imperial coach used to carry Alexandra Feodorovna to her coronation. In yellow gold and translucent strawberry-coloured enamel, the coach, one of the most splendid achievements of the goldsmith's art, is surmounted by the Imperial crown in rose-cut diamonds and six double-headed eagles on the roof; it is fitted with engraved rock crystal windows and platinum tires, and is decorated with a diamond-set trellis in gold and an Imperial eagle in diamonds on either door. It is perfectly articulated, even to the two steps that may be let down when the doors are opened. The interior is enamelled with pale blue curtains behind the upholstered seats and footstool and has a painted ceiling with a turquoise-blue sconce and hook set in the centre. The hook may have once held a tiny egg-shaped, briolette-cut emerald pendant, which is now missing.

Workmaster: Mikhail Perkhin | Assistant: Henrik Wigström | Miniature by Georg Stein.

Marks: M. P. in Cyrillic, 56, crossed anchors and sceptre, Wigström roughly scratched on inner surface of shell, pre-1899 assay mark

Dimensions: Height of egg – 127 mm. (5 in.) | Length of miniature – 93 mm. (3 11/16 in.)

Note: The celebrations following the coronation turned to disaster the next day, when hundreds died, and thousands were injured in a stampede for free beer and coronation souvenirs at Moscow's Khodynka Meadow. Nicholas II followed the poor advice of his uncles and that evening he attended a lavish ball organized by the French ambassador. Ordinary Russians were appalled at what appeared to be a callous disregard of the day's terrible events. Superstitious Russians regarded it as an inauspicious start to the new reign.

Provenance:

April 13 (OS), 1897 Presented to Alexandra Feodorovna, a gift from Nicholas II; cost 5,650 silver roubles (included the cost for a display case billed at 150 silver roubles)

April 10 (OS), 1909. Housed in Alexandra Feodorovna's study at the Winter Palace

September 16-20 (OS), 1917. One of forty or so eggs sent to the Armoury Palace of the Kremlin in Moscow by the Kerensky Provisional Government for safekeeping

February-March 1922. Transferred to the Sovnarkom, the Council of People's Commissars

ca. 1925. Transferred to the Antikvariat

ca. 1927. One of nine Imperial eggs sold by the Antikvariat, Moscow, to Emanuel Snowman of Wartski

1934. Transferred from Wartski, Llandudno, Wales, to Wartski, London, having been purchased for £600.

May 19, 1934. Bought by Charles Parsons, London for £1,500

June 1935. Sold back to Wartski, London, by Charles Parsons who was unable to settle his account.

Sold to Arthur Bradshaw in June 1935 for £1,900

Returned to Wartski 1939 on AEB's death, and became part of their collection

March 29, 1979. Sold by Wartski to Forbes Magazine Collection, New York for £532,000

February 2004. Sold privately as part of the Forbes Magazine Collection, New York, to Russian oil tycoon Viktor Vekselberg, the complete collection costing just over $100 million, according to the purchaser.

November 19, 2013. Fabergé Museum, St. Petersburg, Russia

The Bay Tree Egg (1911)

a.k.a. the Orange Tree Egg until the discovery of the original Fabergé invoice listing it as a Bay tree.

The tree has four main branches that rise from the naturalistically chased gold trunk and divide into smaller branches to hold the nephrite leaves, each finely carved with veining and with a socket at the back into which fits the gold twig. The flowers of white enamel have diamond centres; the buds, rose-cut diamonds; and the fruits are pale rubies and champagne diamonds.

The top third of the tree contains the movement for the singing bird, which emerges from the top of the tree when a jewelled fruit is pressed. It then moves its head from side to side, flaps its wings, and opens its beak and sings. The bird returns to a gold filigree recess inside the top of the egg.

The tub is of white Mexican onyx overlaid by a gold trelliswork enriched with enamelled green swags set with cabochon rubies and pearl finials at the corners. The whole stands upon a nephrite base, the nephrite posts at the corners being applied with spiral bands of gold foliage and connected by free-swinging swags of enamelled green husks and pearls (Chapuis & Droz, 1949; Waterfield & Forbes, 1978; Fabergé, Proler & Skurlov, 1997).

Workmaster: Unknown

Marks: Fabergé, 1911 on front bottom edge of tub, 2990 & kmm II scratched on egg

Materials: Egg, gold, translucent green and opaque white enamel, nephrite, diamonds, rubies, pearls, white Mexican onyx | Miniature songbird – hummingbird feathers.

Dimensions: Height of egg – 273 mm. (10 1/2 in.) | Height of egg (open) – 300 mm. (11 3/4 in.) | Height of case – 327 mm. (12 7/8 in.)

The egg has a fitted red morocco case, the exterior of which is stamped in gold with the initials A. G. H. (Editor's note: Allan G. Hughes, one of the early post-Romanov owners).

This egg has had immense popular appeal, and it has been owned by more people than any other Fabergé egg, Imperial or otherwise. It has had almost a dozen known owners in its time. Its early description, as a bay tree in the Belgrave Square Exhibition catalogue of June 4, 1935, was changed to orange tree in the Sotheby's (London) Auction Catalogue of Valuable Jewels, Jewellery, Etc...*An Imperial Russian Easter Gift by Fabergé*, of July 10, 1947. However, Fabergé's original bill indicates that it is a miniature bay tree. (More details, *Fabergé Research Newsletter*, Spring and Summer 2017)

Provenance:

April 10 (OS), 1911. Presented to Marie Feodorovna, a gift from Nicholas II; cost 12,800 roubles. Probably housed at the Anichkov Palace

September 16-20 (OS), 1917. One of forty or so eggs sent to the Armoury Palace of the Kremlin in Moscow by the Kerensky Provisional Government for safekeeping

February-March 1922. Transferred to the Sovnarkom, the Council of People's Commissars

ca. 1925. Transferred to the Antikvariat (Trade Department)

ca. 1927. One of nine Imperial eggs sold by the Antikvariat, Moscow, to Emanuel Snowman of Wartski

May 11, 1928. Released from the State Repository as a prospective gift for the Shah of Persia. Returned the following September

March 12, 1934. Transferred from Wartski, Llandudno, Wales for Wartski, London, valued at £950

1934. Sold by Wartski for £950, **probably** to Allan G. Hughes

June 1935. Owned by Allan G. Hughes, London

According to Geoffrey Munn, it was sold to AEB in November 1935 with eight other pieces for £2,555

Owned by W. Magalow

July 10, 1947. Lot 53 sold by Sotheby's (London) from the Collection of Lilian, Lady Cadman, widow of British Petroleum executive Sir John Cadman, to buyer's agent Collins for £1,650 (£1,500 plus 10 percent buyer's premium); $6,600. Collins acted on behalf of Wartski, London

1949. Owned by Maurice Sandoz, Switzerland

June 1958. Collection of the late Maurice Sandoz

Acquired by A La Vieille Russie, New York, from Sandoz heirs

1962. Private collection, United States

Owned by Mildred Kaplan, New York

July 1965. Sold by Mildred Kaplan for $150,000 to Forbes Magazine Collection, New York

Elsewhere it is noted that Malcolm Forbes paid $35,000 for this Egg.

February 2004. Sold privately as part of the Forbes Magazine Collection, New York, to Viktor Vekselberg.

November 19, 2013. The Fabergé Museum St. Petersburg, Russia

This is a tangled provenance to say the least. There is no explanation for why the Bay Tree Egg does not appear in AEB's inventory. Therefore, according to Kieran McCarthy of Warski, he never owned it. Why then is Geoffrey Munn adamant that it appears on an original bill of sale with other (unspecified) items sold to AEB in November 1935? Is it possible to make a wild guess that AEB had sold or exchanged it with another collector (Magalow) before his death? We do not know if he ever had dealings with anyone other than Wartski, though it is most unlikely so far as Fabergé is concerned. However, it is that *probably* that bothers me, noted in the sale to Allan G. Hughes. Further, the Forbes Magazine Collection Catalogue lists AEB in the provenance way before Geoffrey Munn's book was published.

Another item in Arthur's inventory in the flower studies section reads:

Orange tree, enamel and Jade, in a Pot.

Nicholas II Equestrian Egg, *Apollo*.

Nicholas II Equestrian Egg (1913)

In Arthur's inventory the following appears:

Enamelled Egg, top set with Rubies and Diamonds, with miniature of Tsarina on one side surrounded with Diamonds and diamond set double-headed Eagle on opposite side. Interior containing model of Nicholas 11 on horseback. The dates 1613-1913 in Diamonds commemorate 300 years of Romanoff rule.

Kenneth Snowman, in his book *The Art of Carl Fabergé* (1953), gives a more detailed description and states in his Catalogue of Imperial Eggs:

The Egg was a special gift presented during the Romanov Tercentenary celebrations in 1913 by the Tsarina to her husband. Enamelled pale green on an engraved silver field it is supported on a white onyx and silver gilt pedestal set with rose diamonds. A latticed canopy of brilliant diamonds and cabochon rubies is surmounted by a cabochon emerald which when pressed, causes the two hinged halves of the Egg to fall apart revealing a silver equestrian statue of Nicholas 11 carrying the flag, and standing on a silver road set with rose diamonds to suggest cobbles. On one side is a miniature portrait of the Tsarina bordered by brilliant diamonds, and on the other a magnificent double-headed eagle set in brilliant diamonds with a five-carat canary diamond in the centre. This Egg is unique.

In the Collection of Harry H. Blum Esq. (p.100).

Blum was a Chicago merchant who owned several department stores specialising in ladies' clothing. He was a collector of antiques,

French art, watches, and other objets d'art, and the Equestrian Egg was exhibited as part of his collection at the Art Institute of Chicago in 1949.

Blum died in 1966. The Equestrian Egg did not appear again until Christie's Geneva auction in 1977 when it was sold on April 27, 1977, Lot 481, for SFr 550,000 ($220,000) to Eskander Aryeh of Great Neck, Long Island (NY).

Aryeh, an Iranian real estate developer and collector, commissioned his sister to buy the egg at auction then flew to Geneva to collect it but, when he saw it, he had doubts. He suggested it might be a fake and he refused to pay. Christie's sued him, and the matter was only settled when Kenneth Snowman wrote a letter declaring the Egg to be an authentic Fabergé Imperial Egg. Dr. Geza von Habsburg, internationally renowned author and Fabergé expert who was in charge of that department at Christie's Geneva in 1977, also confirmed the Egg to be genuine. He had joined the firm eleven years before, in 1966, but he relied on the opinion of Kenneth Snowman who was his mentor.

A lawsuit between the auction house and purchaser for refusal to pay the buyer's fee was settled with Aryeh paying $400,000 (including legal fees and interest) for an egg attributed to Fabergé workmaster Viktor Aarne. However, Ulla Tillander-Godenhielm in her 1980 publication, *Carl Fabergé and His Contemporaries*, p. 40, states Aarne (active workmaster 1891-1904) had returned to Finland in 1904 after selling his St. Petersburg workshop and opened his own establishment. Therefore, the Nicholas II Equestrian with a 1913 date could not be Aarne's work. (If the Tsarina wished this gift to the Tsar to be a secret, is it not possible that she may have commissioned Aarne to make the egg *in Finland?*)

In 1985, Aryeh put the Equestrian Egg on the market again, but Christie's New York President Christopher Burge refused to sell it, and it was withdrawn before the auction. At this time more experts were called in; Kenneth Snowman again, who prevaricated and suggested it was not an Imperial Egg but a lesser work – he did not say it was not by Fabergé. From *a la Vieille Russie*, Peter Schaffer claimed it was a fake. Furious with Christie's, his original doubts about the Egg now apparently confirmed, Aryeh sued for the improbable sum of $37,000.000. A protracted battle ensued, during which time Aryeh died, and the matter was finally settled with the family in 1989 for an undisclosed sum.

McCanless, C. *Fabergé and His Works: An Annotated Bibliography of the First Century of His Art*, 1994, includes 27 citations about the authenticity of the egg and the legal wrangling from April 1977-May 1989.

The whereabouts of the Nicholas II Equestrian Egg are unknown, and it has been expunged not just from the catalogue of Imperial Eggs, but from the record. Dr. von Habsburg suggested to me that it could still be in the Christie's vaults. However, repeated requests and a visit to Christie's in New York were all ignored. Also, questions at The Metropolitan Museum of Art in New York and *a la Vieille Russie* drew blank looks. When I mentioned to the lofty gentleman in the latter establishment that I had a family connection I finally caught his attention, and he asked to be informed if I ever found the Equestrian Egg. My response was "get in the queue."

Author's note: Looking for Fabergé fingerprints on this egg, one thing that is apparent is that the covering is much the same design as the Alexander III Equestrian Egg (1910), whose canopy is diamond-set platinum lacework surmounted by a portrait diamond. It also occurs to me that the cobblestones on which the horse stands in the N II Egg have been designed by a master, who else would have used almost invisible rose diamonds to outline the cobblestones? Why would anyone fake Viktor Aarne's mark? The original acquisition of this Egg is not known. Kenneth Snowman (1953) says nothing about its origins. It must be assumed that Emanuel Snowman sold the Egg to Arthur in the belief that it was genuine. Kenneth Snowman, when called in to authenticate the Egg at the 1977 sale to Aryeh, might not have thought it a fake, or could possibly have had doubts but protected Wartski's reputation knowing his father had sold the Egg twice, once to Arthur and then when returned after his death, to Harry Blum, but ten years later he was in no doubt there was something not right about it, the visible hinge being just one example.

Try as I might to fit it into the catalogue of Imperial Eggs so that Arthur could have had one more, when I went to visit the renowned expert Kieran McCarthy and showed him photos of the Equestrian Egg in London in October 2019, his immediate reaction was "it's a fake." He then went on to explain to me why. "For a start," he said, "it looks clumsy, and the canopy is coarsely rendered." I agree with him about the clumsy look, though I had tried to excuse this as there were other Eggs that had an odd look about them. "Then there is the big yellow diamond – this is a modern, brilliant cut stone and that cut was not known before 1919," said Kieran, "therefore it is a post-revolution work and not made in 1913. Nor does it appear in the St. Petersburg stock list of June 1913, which briefly describes seventeen of the Imperial Eggs. Last, but not least, not only had Aarne returned to Finland in 1904, but he did not work on Imperial Eggs, only gold and silver pieces according to Alexander von Solodkoff, and some enamel. (Masterpieces from the house of Fabergé 1984.) "So," said Kieran, "it was a clever and sophisticated thing to do, fake a possible Tercentenary Egg far enough away from the original event, and people were at the time were taken in by it."

As to where the N 11 Egg might be, Kieran took Occam's Razor to the question: "when Christie's refused to sell it," he said, "what could Eskander Aryeh do but take it home?" Does it languish in a corner somewhere, or has it long since been broken up and the big stones sold off? We will probably never know, but I like to imagine that in a casino somewhere in the world, an elderly woman sits at the roulette table, red nails tapping at the edge while the wheel spins and she waits for the ball to drop, a big, canary yellow diamond winking on her finger.

And there the matter might have ended, but the eagle eye of Kieran McCarthy then took another look at Arthur's vast inventory which revealed two more pieces, supposedly commissioned to mark the Romanov Tercentenary, that now fall under suspicion.

Kovsh, jade, enamel and gold handle, set with diamonds and cabochon rubies, dated 1613-1913 by Fabergé.

An Orlitz and Crystal column Thermometer, with enamel and gold mounts, sapphire and diamond crown, with Diamond N.11, and on the reverse a Diamond mounted plaque 1613-1913, commemorating 300 years of Romanoff rule, by Fabergé.

The problem with these household objects is that they are highly unlikely to have been commissioned by the Tsar. A list of Tercentenary souvenirs and jewels, compiled by Roy Tomlin, reveals commemorative medals in gold, silver and bronze, 1.5 million roubles, silver and enamel crosses for the clergy, porcelain plaques with portraits of the Tsar, the Imperial Eagle and dates 1613-1913, postcards, calendars, cups, postage stamps and bric-a-brac. For this event, Fabergé made jewelled presentation gifts: brooches, bracelets, chatelaines, pendants, necklaces, rings, cufflinks, tie pins and cigarette cases, and two known silver plates inscribed to the Grand Duchess Marie Georgievna and her daughter Her Highness Princess Ksenia Georgievna. No Kovsh or thermometer.

At this point, the name of Agathon Fabergé, connoisseur, opportunist, and the second son of Carl, crops up. The Bowe brothers, who ran the London branch of Faberge, had little time for Agathon, and they clearly did not they trust him. Allan Bowe in a letter to his brother Arthur in 1905 writes that Carl had been usurped in the firm by his son Agathon who now "does what he likes…..the young man is a slave to a morbid and wavering character and cannot be depended upon for one minute…Besides this his greed of money passes the bounds of decency, and all is sacrificed to it." (Quoted in Kieran McCarthy, *Fabergé in London.* p.29)

Agathon had joined the family firm in 1895. He had been given the task of cataloguing the Imperial Crown Jewels for the Romanovs in 1914, and it is said he became an expert in the Diamond Room of the Winter Palace. He left the family business in 1916 and was imprisoned by the Bolsheviks during the revolution. He was released in 1921 to work on, photograph and catalogue the Imperial Treasures in the Moscow Armoury, until 1923. He then had an intimate acquaintance with these objects, having worked on them twice. Might this have been the perfect opportunity for him to study, at close quarters and alone, the comparatively small number of Tercentenary objects and contemplate possibly "filling the gaps"? Viktor Aarne in Finland, furnished with photographs, might have constructed the "Tercentenary" Egg, and signed it with his own mark. He certainly made thermometers, and could have made a Kovsh, but would he have gone so far as to sign *Fabergé?* Was there a relationship with Agathon who retired to Helsinki? Aarne worked for Fabergé in St. Petersburg from 1899 to 1904 so he would have known Agathon, and they both ended up in Helsinki. Too much of a coincidence?

This is pure speculation but there is no documentation of how the three supposed Tercentenary objects in Arthur's collection came to Wartski in the first place. There are only a few references to Agathon and his transactions in the literature. Geoffrey Munn in his book, *Wartski the first 150 Years* p.74, wonders under what circumstances Agathon brought the study of three enamelled pansies in a rock crystal pot, to Wartski in May 1937. One detects a note of doubt about the origin of this piece.

Agathon had a close relationship with Henry Bainbridge, Fabergé's London representative and author, and they are pictured together at the famous 1935 Fabergé exhibition in Belgrave Square. However, when Agathon brought the ten hardstone figures of Russian national types to London in 1937 he took them to Wartski, rather than the London branch of Fabergé, who then sold them to Arthur who had previously bought the Man Smoking and the Balalaika Player. He might have brought the fake Tercentenary Egg to London, and if it had not aroused suspicion other objects could have followed. But he might not have risked offering them to Bainbridge.

Note: the other Fabergé work this Egg most resembles is the Alexander III Equestrian Egg, also held in the Kremlin Armoury, where Agathon would have had ample time to examine and photograph it.

The real Tercentenary Egg is in the Kremlin Armoury Museum, Moscow. It is decorated with eighteen portraits of Romanov rulers, framed in diamonds, and contains within a rotating wheel a dark blue enamel globe showing the Russian frontiers.

The Matilda Geddings Gray Foundation Collection, photo courtesy of The Metropolitan Museum of Art, New York.

Basket of Lilies of Valley (1896)

Item No. 17 in the Flowers section of Arthur's inventory reads: *Pearl and diamond Lily-of-the-Valley Sprays, with Jade leaves in Gold Basket, by Fabergé*. This brief description of Fabergé's most celebrated flower study might have been overlooked had it not been for Geoffrey Munn's book which states, firmly, on page 238 that Arthur purchased this basket in 1935 for £1,900.

In his book *Fantasies and Treasures*, (1995) Géza von Habsburg writes: "The firm's most celebrated floral composition, and Empress Alexandra Feodorovna's favourite piece by the master, was the Basket of Lilies of the Valley presented to her by the merchants of Nizhny Novgorod in 1896, which stood on her desk until the Revolution. In this object Fabergé has succeeded in transcending nature, breathing life into inanimate materials, thereby creating an immortal work of art. p.58"

However, not everyone was charmed. When the Lilies of the Valley Basket was exhibited at the 1935 Exhibition of Russian Art, an anonymous critic, clearly not a fan of Fabergé, wrote that it was displayed with other "familiar horrors."

Considered one of the most important Fabergé works in the United States, the woven gold basket holds nineteen individual gold stems emerging from nine plants of lilies of the valley, resting in realistic moss constructed of spun and clipped green and yellow gold, the flowers made of seed pearls and rose cut diamonds with leaves of carved nephrite.

Dimensions H. 7 ½ inches, L. 8 ½ inches

The Basket retains its original presentation case covered in claret velvet and emblazoned with The Empress Alexandra's personal cipher.

Provenance: Wartski; A.E. Bradshaw, Wartski, Hammer Galleries Inc., New York, Matilda Geddings Gray Foundation Collection, New Orleans Museum of Art, but after Hurricane Katrina in 2005 the collection was transferred to the Cheekwood Museum of Art, Nashville, Tennessee; Returned to New Orleans in 2011. On loan to the Metropolitan Museum of Art, New York.

1949 Loan Exhibition of the Works of Carl Fabergé, London

1951 Exhibition at Hammer Galleries, New York, basket on loan, not for sale.

It is worth noting that also in Arthur's inventory, amongst his thirty-nine listed flowers are a two more lilies of the valley carvings: *A Spray of Pearl and Diamond Lily of the Valley with Jade leaf, in Crystal Pot, and a Spray of Moonstone Lilies of the Valley, with Jade leaves, in Crystal Vase.*

Royal Collection Trust/All Rights Reserved.

Spray of Cornflowers, Buttercups, and a Diamond Bee (c.1900)

Item 1 of Arthur's Inventory in the flower section reads: *Spray of Cornflowers and Buttercups, Gold and Enamel, with Diamond set Bee, in Crystal Vase, by Fabergé.* And smaller companion piece.

Arthur owned two other cornflower studies and one of Three Gold and Enamel King Buttercups with Jade leaves in a Crystal Pot (sold at Christies for £350,000 in November 2013). But it is the combination spray that concerns us. Purchased by Arthur early in his collecting, Wartski persuaded him to lend the cornflowers with diamond bee for the *Exhibition of Russian Art* at No. 1 Belgrave Square, in 1935.

The descriptive entry in the Royal Collection Trust reads: Rock crystal, gold, Enamel, rose diamonds, rubies, 22.3 x 14.0 x 8.0 cm

Kenneth Snowman (1979) describes it as follows: *"A spray of buttercups in gold enamelled translucent yellow and green over engraved grounds, and cornflowers enamelled translucent blue with diamond centres, with green gold stalks and leaves in a rock crystal jar. A diamond, ruby and black enamelled bee in red gold is poised on one of the buttercups. Height 9 inches."* (p.127).

Both Cornflower studies were purchased by Queen Elizabeth, the Queen Mother, in 1944 and 1947 respectively, the one with the diamond bee costing £375.

Loaned to Wartski in May 1971 for Exhibition, *A Thousand Years of Enamel*.

Loaned to the V & A in 1977 for an international exhibition celebrating The Queen's Silver Jubilee. Curated by A. Kenneth Snowman.

The Matilda Geddings Gray Foundation Collection, photo courtesy of The Metropolitan Museum of Art, New York.

Loaned to Wartski 1992, *Fabergé from Private Collections* in aid of The Samaritans in Lowestoft.

The Royal Collection.

Fabergé Cigarette Case

Gift of Emanuel Snowman to Arthur, inscribed *"To Arthur E. Bradshaw, a man who radiates happiness and charm. Emanuel Snowman 1935."* The same year as Arthur acquired a great amount of his collection from Wartski.

Described as: *A Silver cigarette case, enamelled translucent lavender guilloché in radiating design, Romanov double-headed eagle in Gold, moonstone push.*

Unfortunately, the family sold this with the rest of Arthur's collection perhaps because, a compulsive smoker, he had died of lung cancer, or just because it was part of the Fabergé collection and much disliked by Evelyn. It now belongs to the Matilda Geddings Gray Foundation Collection, New Orleans Museum of Art, on loan to the Metropolitan Museum of Art, New York.

Catherine the Great Sedan Chair

The first Russian treasure acquired by Wartski in 1927 comprised about eighty items, one of which was the Catherine the Great Sedan Chair which seemed even then, according to an early photo, to have parted company with the Imperial Catherine the Great Egg of 1914, also known as the Grisaille Egg, also known as The Pink Cameo Egg. It was said to be the "surprise" in this Egg, now in the Hillwood Museum in Washington D.C. However, when the chair was tested it did not fit the Egg at Hillwood because it was assumed to be too big. In fact, according to Kieran McCarthy who sits on the advisory board of the Fabergé museum in St. Petersburg, it fits perfectly, if very snugly, and has since been recognised as the missing "surprise."

A mechanical sedan chair in engraved red gold with green gold acanthus borders, enamelled translucent yellow over a ground engraved with Romanov double-headed eagles. Rock crystal panels, inside a miniature gold figure of Catherine the Great in ermine cloak, rose diamond crown. The chair is carried by two court Arabs in gold and scarlet enamel, a small gold key winds the clockwork mechanism enabling them to walk forward naturalistically. Signed HW. Length: 3¼ inches.

The Catherine the Great sedan chair returned to Wartski after Arthur's death. It eventually found its way into the Forbes collection and is now in the St. Petersburg museum.

The Balalaika Player

A Peasant (mujik) in grey jasper, lapis lazuli, cacholong (a form of opal) and orlitz, sapphire eyes, hair and moustache in coffee jasper, seat in Siberian jasper and balalaika in silver gilt. Marked H.W. and engraved Fabergé. This appears in Arthur's inventory as:

Figure of Harmonist, in various stones, by Fabergé.

Height 4 ½ inches.

In all there are ten hardstone figures in his inventory. All are illustrated in the *Connoisseur* April 1938 in an article by H.C. Bainbridge.

Geoffrey Munn reported that "The now-famous 'Balalaika Player' entered Wartski's London stock from the Llandudno branch, described as "Vari-stone harmonist' on 2 February 1935, with a cost price of £60.1s.6d, and was sold to Bradshaw a week later for £350."

In 1937 Arthur bought another eight hardstone figures and paid £7,777 for them, along with other goods.

Following Arthur's death, the figures were back at Wartski on sale for 1,100 and were sold in July 1941 to Sir William Seeds for £1,800.

After his death, when a buyer for the whole group could not be found, it was decided to break it up and offer each figure separately.

In 1975 the Balalaika Player was sold for £19,000 and five years later it was auctioned by Christies, Geneva for 425,000 Swiss francs, the equivalent of nearly £100,000

The figure is in the Museum Collection in Moscow.

G. Munn, *Wartski the first one hundred and fifty years.* pp.66-67 ill. pp. 68-69 *Connoisseur* April 1938

Other Fabergé items of interest included:

Ostrich

Seated bird, agate, with gold feet and diamond eyes. GM ill. p 238 (AB # 247)

On one occasion, in September 1935, Arthur bought a large consignment of eighty-seven carved animals for £800. The following November, Wartski purchased another collection of 100 carved stone animals from the dealer Popoff in Paris which Arthur bought in its entirety for £2,750 on December 12, 1936.

Geoffrey Munn wrote that by now Arthur owned more than 220 hardstone carvings of animals, "possibly the largest collection ever made following the Russian Revolution." An advertisement for the group of 100 states that the animals came from the Russian Imperial Family collection, and included: a seated pig with diamond eyes, a frog with cabochon ruby eyes and a mouth of rose cut diamonds, bears, dachshunds, a bulldog, roosters, more pigs, ducks and a hippopotamus. There were numerous rabbits too, and a nephrite Tyrannosaurus rex, a study of four sleeping pigs in agate, and another of four puppies asleep on a rug.

Other unique Fabergé items owned by Arthur included: a solid 18ct. gold coffee set weighing 1,411 grammes comprising Coffee Pot, Sugar basin, Cream jug, and Tongs on a Tray, (the objects are surprisingly small and also surprisingly heavy) a unique miniature tambourine made of gold, enamel, pearl and agate, an enamelled gold convolvulus, and a hardstone cactus.

In the fifty-page inventory of Arthur's collection some of the entries are so brief – sometimes just two words, as to be almost incomprehensible. One can imagine two of Wartski's staff sitting at the dining room table in The Grange, taking each of the 800 odd items from his display cases, noting and returning them.

Turkey, fancy stone

Elephant rose quartz. (Arthur owned fifty-five elephants).

Owl, topaz

Silver cabbage

This gives one some idea of brevity. Then there are other items described in the sort of detail that instantly forms a picture and would be easy to recognise.

Square silver striking and alarm Clock, dial surrounded by rubies and with ruby set Coronet and F.S.E. on top, by Fabergé.

Spray of four White Chalcedony flowers, with two Jade leaves, enamel and silver pot and emerald water.

Oblong Jade Box, by Fabergé. with miniature of Alexander 11, with ruby and diamond crown surrounded by diamonds.

Ribbed gold cigarette Case with large diamond Imperial Crest in circle on top, diamond thumb piece, and fitted with cabochon Sapphire topped Gold Pencil.

There were hundreds of other items displayed in the dining room at The Grange in glass-fronted cases, but without images, I have decided to include only the most well-known pieces. It is a matter of profound regret for the family that the collection was broken up and sold off. A few bits and pieces of jewellery, silver, and carved animals remain in their hands but none, alas, by Fabergé; the animals are of Chinese origin, and the jewellery consists of a few diamonds set in a ring and Loveday's birthday bracelet, the thing that first drew Arthur to Wartski's window in February 1935.

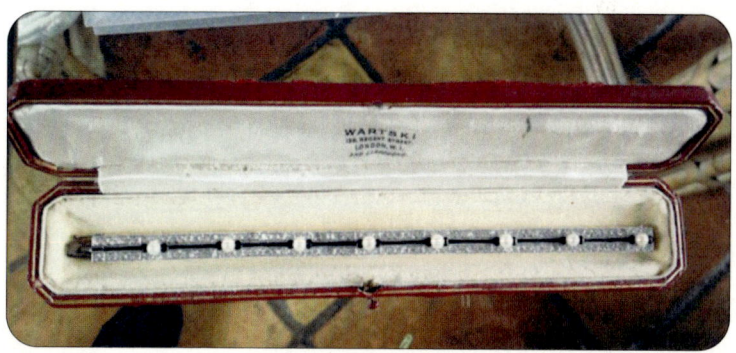

From a private collection

Bibliography

Helme, Nigel, *Thomas Major Cullinan, a biography* (1974) McGraw-Hill.

Keefe, John Webster, *Masterpieces of Fabergé: The Matilda Geddings Grey Foundation Collection* (2008) Cheekwood Botanical Gardens & Museum of Art, Nashville.

McCanless, Christel Ludewig, *Fabergé and His Works; An Annotated Bibliography of the First Century of His Art* (1994) The Scarecrow Press.

McCarthy, Kieran, *Fabergé in London: The British Branch of the Imperial Russian Goldsmith* (2017) ACC Art Books, Woodbridge. UK

Munn, Geoffrey, *Wartski, The First One Hundred and Fifty Years* (2015) Antique Collectors' Club.

Pevsner, N. & Sherwood, J. *The Buildings of England: Oxfordshire* (1974) Yale U.P.

Snowman, A. Kenneth, *The Art of Carl Fabergé* (1953) Faber & Faber.

Snowman, A. Kenneth, *Carl Fabergé Goldsmith to the Imperial Court of Russia* (1979) The Viking Press, N.Y.

Tillander-Godenhielm, Ulla, *The Russian Imperial Reward System during the Reign of Nicholas 11 1894-1917* (2005) Finnish Antiquarian Society, Helsinki.

Thomson, D.H., *Five Miles from Town, the story of the Olympic Sports Club (1968)* Olympic Sports Club.

von Habsburg, Geza, (Archduke) *Fabergé Fantasies and Treasures* (1996) Universe Publishing.

von Solodkoff, Alexander, et al., *Masterpieces from the House of Fabergé* (1984) Abradale Press.

Journals and Catalogues

Apollo, April 1977 p.36

The Connoisseur, April 1938 pp. 200–204

Celebrating the Romanov Tercentenary with Fabergé Imperial Presentation Gifts: A Review. Fabergé Research Newsletter, Fall 2012.

Valuable and Important *objets de vertu* by Carl Fabergé from the Lansdell K. Christie Collection, 1967 Auction catalogue

Sotheby's London; *Sale catalogue for 13 July 1950*, Property of the late Mrs Bradshaw Lots 88,89,90 & 93

Family notes

Dr Hodges issued Arthur's death certificate; it stated the cause was 'carcinoma of the lung.' No surprises there. He left slightly more than 60,000 pounds and a priceless collection by Fabergé and other makers. His funeral was reported at length in The Banbury Advertiser, of 2nd November 1939.

At the December meeting of the Parish council, Arthur's death, after months of severe illness, was noted and the members stood in silence to pay their respects.

For much of the information about the house and family following Arthur's death, I am deeply indebted to Loveday's son Dick Burleston b. 1941 who spent much of his childhood at the Grange.

The Grange continued to be run as a farm after Arthur's death, employing many people in the village and, with a small herd of Jersey cows, the dairy remained active for many years. Richard's huge collection of weapons from the south African wars still hung in the downstairs hall. These went in a clearing sale after Evelyn's death, along with the Union Jack.

Evelyn returned Arthur's collection to Wartski following his death, keeping only four pieces of table silver for her own use. She lived on at The Grange, with her lifelong friend Aileen Rutledge as her companion, until she died in 1950. The death duties were so huge that the Grange had to be sold to a developer and now consists of a forty dwelling housing estate. The main house is divided into three apartments. Some cottages, the greenhouse, the original stone wall, and a large field bordered by the woodland where the poly walk was, still exist.

After Evelyn's death, Ailey went to live with Loveday and her family in Yorkshire, and when Loveday left to move to the south, Ailey retired to Swanage.

Kate Sale stayed in Folkestone after Rolly died, surviving the bombardments of WW2, with visits to Evelyn at The Grange until her death in 1952. She left just ten thousand pounds between the two daughters and her solicitor. All her children outlived her, and John Walker Sale remained in the army and was awarded an OBE.

Both John Bradshaw and his wife are buried in the Walker family vault of Christ Church, Southgate, not at Steeple Aston. He left an estate of over 381,000 pounds. The Grange was demolished, and the lovely gardens are now a public park. There is a John Bradshaw road in Southgate.

Stewart Bradshaw did not remarry; he died in 1946.

Harry Bradshaw's widow Agnes died in 1955, and the daughter, Elinor Agnes, who married several times, in 1981.

Evelyn Loveday m. Bryan Burleston in 1940; he was killed in the war in 1941 leaving a son, Bryan (Dick) Burleston b. 1941. She married again, to Alexander Dunstan Sharp, and had a son Robert Dunstan Sharp, b. 1948.

Kathleen Eira m. James Anthony Hibbert and had four children: Christopher James Bradshaw b. 1950, Carolyn Claire b. 1952, Vivien Eira b. 1953 and Gillian Frances b. 1961.

Richard Edward "Bobby" Bradshaw, a distinguished and daring flying ace during the war, m. Margaret Monument. Both died in a car crash in 1958 leaving Sarah Evelyn, b. 1952 and Harry Stephen b. 1955.

Vivien Stals has recently published a fascinating, illustrated monograph on Arthur's father, Vice-Admiral Richard Bradshaw. Hopefully, it will be available online in the future. More information about Loveday, Eira and Bobby is found in the family tree, with photographs.